His brief burst of laughter made her jump.

'Wouldn't you know it?' Sam's tone was tinged with bitterness and she was glad she couldn't see his face. 'We parted company nearly two years ago and we're still doing the same things, making the same decisions. . .' His voice tailed off and she knew he was remembering the time their decisions had put them at cross purposes; knew he was remembering that he had sworn never to forgive her.

Sian squeezed her eyes tight shut and buried her face in the pillow, determined not to cry again. She had cried enough over Sam Forrester.

Josie Metcalfe lives in Cornwall now with her long-suffering husband, four children and two horses, but when she was an Army brat, frequently on the move, books became the only friends who came with her wherever she went. Now that she writes them herself she is making new friends and hates saying goodbye at the end of a book—but there are always more characters in her head clamouring for attention until she can't wait to tell their stories.

SEEING EYE TO EYE

BY

JOSIE METCALFE

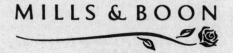

MILLS & BOON

MILLS & BOON, the Rose Device and LOVE ON CALL are trademarks of the publisher.
Harlequin Mills & Boon Limited,
Eton House, 18–24 Paradise Road, Richmond, Surrey TW9 1SR
This edition published by arrangement with
Harlequin Enterprises B.V.

© Josie Metcalfe 1995

ISBN 0 263 79261 7

Set in 10 on 12 pt Linotron Times
03-9508-53703

Typeset in Great Britain by CentraCet, Cambridge
Made and printed in Great Britain

AUTHOR'S NOTE

ORBIS is an international organisation dedicated to saving sight across the world through education. The primary vehicle for Orbis's work is a converted DC-10 jet housing a complete eye hospital and teaching facility. Since 1982 the Orbis aircraft has visited more than 70 countries to provide in-service training for ophthalmic surgeons, nurses, community health workers and technicians. As a result of these efforts, together with a number of other similar Orbis-funded programmes without the aircraft, over 28,000 doctors, nurses and other health-care workers are now using new skills to benefit countless individuals afflicted by visual impairment.

CHAPTER ONE

'ONE of the surgeons has had a car crash!'

The bald announcement silenced the usual babble of sounds in the busy London office of Orbis International.

'Not one of the ones due to fly to Beijing?' The question was filled with horror. 'That only leaves us with a couple of days to arrange a replacement ophthalmologist, and we already had a vacancy on that flight.'

'How is he?' one small voice queried, and the rest had the grace to look discomfited.

'It wasn't serious, and his secretary said he'll sign up for an alternative venue as soon as he can. In the meantime. . .'

There was frantic activity for a while, with faxes flying between London, New York, Hong Kong and Houston before the problem was solved.

'Eureka!' The fax was waved aloft. 'Look up Forrester on the register. It's a fairly recent addition—volunteered for the next trip but willing to slot in earlier if necessary.'

Keys were tapped swiftly and efficiently on the other side of the room and the display came up on the screen.

'Forrester. . . Forrester. . . Ah, here it is. S. Forrester. Trained in London. Five years' experience. . .'

'Right, get a message off to find out whether two days' notice is enough, then send confirmation to the other offices and the frontwork team in Beijing. In the meantime, keep your fingers crossed!'

* * *

Sian Forrester dropped her bags full of shopping just inside the sitting-room door and kicked her shoes off before she flopped back on to the settee clutching a handful of papers.

'I must be mad,' she muttered, running the neatly manicured fingers of one hand through short dark curly hair and shaking her head as she leafed through he papers again. 'In three days I'll be in Beijing!'

She looked out of the window at the fading light of an early summer day and grimaced at the blustery rain. 'At least it's on the same latitude as Madrid, so the weather should be a bit better than this.'

That thought was enough to have her scrambling to her feet as she remembered the amount of sorting and packing she had to do. She had dashed out to look for lighter clothing for every day use and any possible sightseeing, and had been pleased with her choices.

Multitudinous pieces of paper had flown to and fro today, some apparently disappearing into thin air.

She had, however, been warned that there would be various official receptions and entertainments with which the host country would honour their visitors.

She had wondered whether she ought to buy some more formal dresses especially for the trip, but dismissed the idea. She already had several beautiful ones which had been lurking unworn in the back of her wardrobe ever since she had bought them nearly two years ago.

Two years. . .

That realisation brought her up short. Was it really two years since she and Sam had come to the parting of the ways? Two years since he had made his terrible accusation. . .?

She pressed her soft lips together angrily, annoyed

that even after all this time Sam could intrude on her
thoughts and feelings. Ruthlessly banishing him to the
darkest corners of her mind, she determined to concentrate on the essential tasks ahead of her.

Ever since she had volunteered her services to Orbis
International she had started to make preparations, and
had managed to amass a small store of instruments and
surgical supplies which she was intending to take with
her, and several sets of slides and notes detailing the
surgical work she routinely performed and the methods
she had developed.

Some of the equipment would need careful packing
for the long journey, so the sooner she started, the
sooner she would be able to get some much-needed rest.

She retrieved her check-list and ran a finger down
each item.

'Lucky I'd had my jabs early,' she muttered, wincing
at the memory of the cocktail of yellow fever and the
two strains of hepatitis, then clicked her fingers and
reached for the two containers of malaria tablets. She
cast a quick eye over the instructions again to confirm
the dosage, and checked that she would have sufficient
for the time she would be away.

A squadron of butterflies took off inside her each
time she allowed herself to think about her destination.

Beijing, capital of China—and she'd be there in less
than three days!

As the plane came in to land, Sian swallowed to relieve
the pressure in her ears and gathered her belongings on
her lap. She was already more than an hour late because
of rough weather and didn't want to be the cause of any
further delay for the poor person who had been detailed
to meet her flight.

Half an hour later she was still waiting for someone to come forward to identify himself as a representative of Orbis International. Her second massive yawn reminded her that her body didn't know what time it was, never mind what day, and she marched up to the information desk with her documents at the ready.

She was ready for a frustrating battle in an unknown language, and was delighted that just the mention of the word Orbis brought smiling helpfulness and the arrival of a taxi to deliver her to her hotel.

Sian was amazed when she realised where she had been brought, the first-class hotel being way beyond what she had been expecting.

'I have come to join Orbis International. . .'

Once again she had uttered the magic words and she was whisked through the formalities of registration and up to a room which seemed the height of luxury. She gazed longingly at the beautiful twin beds, each the size of a normal double bed, and nearly gave in to the urge to curl up and sleep.

After the young man had left her bags on the stand at the foot of one of the beds and closed the door softly behind him, Sian stood and looked around.

She had remembered belatedly that some of the giant hotel chains were very generous with reduced rates and even free accommodation for the staff of Orbis, knowing that the whole operation depended on volunteers and charity for its existence.

There was another suitcase on the stand by the other bed, and the scent of soap in the air when she went to check the adjoining bathroom.

'I wonder who my room-mate is?' she pondered aloud as she glanced about. 'She's very tidy—not a thing out of place except. . .' She reached out to pick up a small sheaf of papers and recognised her own name on them.

A quick look confirmed that they were a brief itinerary for this evening, and a rapid glance at her watch made her groan aloud.

'Still set on London time,' she berated herself, wondering how much time she had before the crew meeting at which the visiting faculty was due to be introduced. 'I don't even know if I've arrived in time for a meal.'

She flew into action, well accustomed to washing and dressing in a hurry when the situation demanded and, although she still missed the shining river of dark hair which she had ruthlessly removed nearly two years ago, she was grateful for the ease with which her present style could be managed.

Her dark blue eyes were surrounded by lashes so thick and dark that they needed no enhancement, and she contented herself with a soft touch of colour on her lips before she tucked her belongings neatly away in the drawer.

'Right.' She picked up her small document-case and slipped the papers inside. 'Let's find out what happens next.'

She tucked the key in the pocket of her loosely pleated cream trousers and straightened the hem of the long-line jacket before she turned and made her way along the lushly decorated corridor to the bank of lifts.

The clock on the wall above the lift doors nearly made her scream. Not only had she missed her meal, but she was going to be late if it took more than four minutes to find the small conference-room where the rest of the group was meeting.

After the lift attendant had given her excruciatingly precise directions, she reached the double doors at the

first attempt and paused outside, taking a deep breath
to still the quivering which still assailed her at inopportune moments. She could hear the distinctive hum of
conversation in the room beyond, and stiffened her
spine to combat the shyness which had so often prevented her from speaking her mind in the past.

She opened the door just as the mission manager
called for attention, and Sian gave a little sigh of relief
that her entry had gone unnoticed as the other members
of the group were now facing in the other direction. She
slid silently into the nearest chair and relaxed, taking
the opportunity to glance around at the assembled
group.

'The field staff consists of twenty-five,' the mission
manager was saying. 'When we add the visiting staff,
the number can be up to forty but, in spite of this, the
Orbis team works well together because we make a
point of being a team.' She paused and glanced down at
a sheaf of notes before she smiled around at the
assembled group. 'I would like everyone to welcome
our visitors, so I will call out your names. If you will
stand or raise your hand, we can start to learn who you
are.'

Sian's stomach clenched in a familiar way although
she knew the reaction no longer showed on her face.
She had worked hard to control her visible vulnerability
and now hid it under a smooth mask of serenity as her
turn approached.

'Forrester.' The sound of her name jerked her out of
her thoughts and she stood awkwardly, just as a long
tanned male arm was raised, with the accompanying
deep voice, saying, 'Here.'

There was a startled silence as they each turned
towards the other. Sian felt her face heating as, out of

the corner of her eye, she saw all the heads turn towards them.

Her own gaze was fixed on the piercing dark eyes which had swivelled towards her.

'Sam,' she whispered soundlessly, and felt the blood drain out of her face and her limbs lose their strength so that it was a miracle she was still standing.

For long seconds their eyes meshed, and it was as if they were the only people in the room.

After the first shock, it seemed as if an expression of pleasure had crossed his face, but it was so brief that Sian was sure she must have imagined it.

'Excuse me?'

They both jerked when the insistent voice broke in on their isolation.

'Which one of you is Dr Forrester?'

Sam raised one wry eyebrow, then turned towards the puzzled manager.

'Both of us,' he confirmed, and Sian recognised of old the underlying humour in his tone.

'Oh.' The poor woman was obviously nonplussed. 'Well, which one is S. Forrester?'

'Both of us,' he repeated, the laughter more evident this time and drawing a chuckle from some of their audience.

The manager glanced down at her notes, then looked from one to the other, her puzzlement growing.

'Which one trained at——?'

Sam interrupted gently.

'It might help to sort matters out a little if I tell you that we both trained at the same hospital at the same time, but as to how we both ended up here together when you were only expecting one of us, I don't know.'

He glanced briefly back at Sian before he continued, 'Does it create a problem?'

'Well, no. I don't think so. Unless. . . Are you offering the same speciality? That would make a difference in organising the selection of patients tomorrow morning.'

'I was expecting to do anterior segment work. . .' He turned and invited Sian to speak with a gesture of his hand.

'I specialise in paediatric work,' she announced quietly, and was startled by the flash of anger which crossed Sam's face.

'In which case there's no problem at all,' the manager confirmed happily. 'I'll just have to make sure that my bulletins make it clear which of you is which, and check that your entries on the register are amended so that this doesn't happen again.'

Her voice was relieved as she moved on to complete her round of introductions, not knowing the turmoil she had left in her wake.

Suddenly it dawned on Sian that for the next week she would be thrown into close contact with Sam for the first time in nearly two years.

Without her permission, her eyes drifted across the other members of the team towards him and stayed. They greedily took in the dark silkiness of his hair and the breadth of his shoulders clothed in a fine cotton shirt, the short sleeves revealing the hair-sprinkled strength of his muscular arms.

Her eyes prickled ominously as she was overwhelmed by the memory of how gently that strength could be tempered; how superb the degree of control Sam could exert over his body while he was in an operating theatre and afterwards, when he was out of it. . .

She pulled herself up short. This was not the way to go about controlling her emotions. The whole situation was just an appalling coincidence. Without the computer mix-up she and Sam would probably never have met again, in spite of all they had once meant to each other.

Sian forced herself to concentrate as the mission manager detailed the system they would follow in the morning.

'We'll be leaving the hotel at half-past seven each day,' she announced to good-humoured groans. 'Of course, that means you'll have to have finished your breakfast by then, because the rest of the meals can be more than a bit haphazard, depending on the schedule.

'The visiting faculty members will be going to a local hospital tomorrow morning with a complement of nurses and fellows—that's what we call the staff ophthalmologists—and they will be accompanied by an administrator. The host doctors have set up screenings for the selection of possible operative cases.

'As you will appreciate, these will be valuable opportunities to discuss examination techniques and so on, as well as for choosing good teaching cases for surgery.'

As she finished her presentation there was a buzz of conversation before she spoke again.

'Are there any questions so far?'

One of the volunteer nurses raised her hand.

'Will there be some sort of meeting tomorrow, after we get back to the hotel, to report back?'

'Certainly,' she confirmed. 'We hope to have every-one back here by four of five at the latest—including the rest of the team, who will have been preparing the plane. You'll be free to relax and eat until seven, when we'll have a crew meeting. It usually develops into a real brain-storming session and can last for an hour or two.' She looked around in case there were any further queries, then nodded.

'Right, then. That's it for now. I'll make sure you're notified of updates on the buses in the morning, including any official functions in the next day or two.'

Having missed her chance to meet her temporary colleagues before the meeting, Sian was loath to deny herself the opportunity just because Sam was in the room.

'Philip?' She introduced herself to the other visiting surgeon, unhappily conscious that she was keeping an unobtrusive eye on Sam. 'I'm Sian Forrester.' She held out her hand.

'Sian?' he queried, as he engulfed her hand in his. 'That's the name of a Chinese city, isn't it? Near where they found the emperor's terracotta army?'

'It depends on your spelling,' she laughed. 'Actually, mine is Welsh for Jane.'

'You don't sound Welsh,' he objected.

'No,' she smiled. 'The connection is several generations back, but my mother wanted to keep it up.'

They chatted for a few minutes, comparing notes on a variety of subjects, before Sian was suddenly overtaken by a huge yawn.

'Oh, I'm so sorry,' she apologised immediately.

'I can take a hint,' Philip laughed.

'No, I didn't——'

'Sian, it's all right. I was only teasing.' He patted her shoulder in a brotherly way. 'We're all pretty tired—due to excitement as much as anything, I think. I'll see you in the morning.'

Sian caught herself glancing across the room one last time before she left, and her heart plummeted into her elegant low-heeled shoes as she realised that Sam had already gone.

All the way back to her room she berated herself for caring that he hadn't said anything to her.

Their—association—had ended nearly two years ago when he had made his vile accusation, but he could at least have made the effort to speak, if only for appearances' sake.

She let herself into her room with the key and stopped just inside the door.

Her room-mate had obviously returned before her and, if the sound of running water was anything to go by, had taken the opportunity to have a shower. Sian sat down on the side of the bed and contemplated her options while she set her travelling alarm for the morning.

She glanced at the menu available from room service and yawned again.

'It's no good,' she muttered, then paused as another huge yawn overtook her. 'I've got to get some sleep. . .' She took a Swiss cotton nightdress out of the drawer and undressed swiftly, hanging her trousers and jacket neatly away beside a fresh peach-coloured blouse ready for the morning, before she slid between blissfully smooth cool sheets.

'I'll brush my teeth as soon as the bathroom's free. . .' she muttered, as her thick dark lashes drooped to meet her prominent cheekbones.

'What the hell. . .!'

The deep voice intruded on her slumbers and Sian's eyebrows drew together.

'No. . .' she murmured indistinctly, rolling her head

against the pillow. She didn't want the nightmare to come back. Not again.

'What are you doing here?'

The voice was louder. Closer. Sam's voice. And Sam's hand shaking her shoulder. That had never happened in her nightmare before.

'Sian!' Her shoulder was shaken again and she started to surface slowly, her eyes opening drowsily as she realised that none of it was a dream.

'Sam?' She blinked up at him as he loomed over her, six feet plus of irate male, his dark robe gaping open to reveal the once-familiar sight of his broad, muscular chest.

Sian struggled to sit up, her sleepiness making every movement an effort.

The bedcovers slithered off her shoulders and landed in her lap, leaving her clothed in a minimal amount of almost sheer fabric.

Sian saw Sam's expression change as he saw how little she was wearing, and deep inside she felt an answering sharp twist of arousal as she watched his pupils dilate.

His hands were clenched into fists at his sides, his knuckles whitening as she sat mesmerised by his presence.

'Sam!' A tide of colour swept up from the revealing cut of her scanty attire as she realised that she had been allowing him to look his fill.

She grasped the edge of the sheet and pulled it up to cover her nightdress modestly. 'What are you doing in here?' She glanced towards the bathroom, expecting to hear the sounds of her room-mate, but the door was open and the room was in darkness.

Suddenly, she realised the significance of what he was

wearing and the full implications hit her like a hurricane.

'No!' She shook her head, the soft dark curls flying. 'Oh, no, you don't.'

She slid her feet out of the covers and reached one hand for the wrap she had left on the arm of the chair. She kept her eyes on him as she thrust her hands into the sleeves and tied the belt viciously tightly.

'I don't know what you think this was supposed to achieve, but I'm not going to share a room with you. You can just go and tell whoever you exchanged with that you've changed your mind.' She glared at him, her arms folded closely around her waist.

Several expressions chased each other across his face before a smile slowly took over.

'I would say the boot was on the other foot, my love.' He drawled the old familiar endearment softly, ironically, as he stepped across to sit on the other bed, swinging his long legs up as he leant easily against the headboard.

'What do you mean?' she questioned uneasily, her eyes focusing on the dark furring on his shins and following the damp swirls up his thighs to where the fabric had slid apart as he sat down.

One lean hand came across to grasp the edge of the fabric, and for a fraction of a second Sian wasn't certain whether he was going to cover himself again or. . .

She blinked and dragged her eyes away, unfortunately meeting the darkly gleaming humour in his frank gaze.

'As I was saying,' he continued, smoothing the robe across his taut thighs. 'I arrived at the hotel about six hours ago and was allocated this room——'

'But *I* was brought to the room not half an hour before the staff meeting. . .'

'Exactly,' he purred. 'So how did you manage to persuade the staff at Reception to let you share my room? Bribery?'

'What?' Her voice emerged as a breathless shriek. 'I didn't even know you were in China, let alone in the same hotel!'

'Well, what a coincidence.' He smiled lazily. 'So, what are we going to do about it?'

'Obviously, you're going to have to find another room,' Sian pronounced with a decisive nod, then wished she hadn't as the muzzy feeling of jet-lag gave a heavy thump. She pinched the bridge of her nose before massaging the hypersensitive skin at her temples.

'That's hardly feasible when Orbis has been allowed special rates on the accommodation.'

'What about sharing with Philip?' She could hear the desperation beginning to creep into her voice.

'I hardly think his wife is going to like that much!' he laughed.

'Oh.' Her shoulders slumped as she looked longingly at the soft pillows and fine cotton sheets.

'Look, Sian, there's obviously not much we can do about this tonight, so why don't you go back to sleep and we'll sort it out in the morning?' He raised one eyebrow and his voice hardened. 'After all, it's not as if we're strangers, is it?'

'No,' she retorted, stung by his tone. 'But we hardly qualify as friends, either.' She winced as her head pounded.

'Hardly!' he agreed coldly, raking her quivering body with a scathing glance. 'Oh, for goodness' sake, get into bed and go to sleep. It's going to be a long hard day tomorrow, and at this rate you're not going to be much use to anyone. . .' He rolled away from her to stand at the other side of his bed, where he proceeded to remove his robe.

Sian gave an audible gasp of surprise at his audacity.

He turned sharply at the sound and, before she could command her eyes to look away, she was made only too aware that Sam was still the best-looking man she had ever seen.

She dragged her eyes up over the taut leanness of his stomach, following the line of dark hair as it widened out towards the coppery discs of his nipples and up towards his shoulders.

He planted one fist on each hip.

'If you're sure you've seen enough. . .' Sam's voice was strangely husky, and she felt her cheeks flaming as she whirled away to loosen the tie of her wrap before sliding quickly into bed.

She hadn't dared to look at his face. She had fought hard to learn to control her expressions, but she knew he would have seen that he still had the same effect on her as he had from the first day they'd met.

Sian snuggled down against the pillow, then lay still, listening to Sam as he settled himself and grateful that he couldn't read her mind.

She wondered if the last two years had changed him at all. Oh, he was still as physically compelling as ever — perhaps more so. She couldn't remember his having quite such muscles two years ago, and wondered if he had taken up weight training.

'Swimming and weight training.' The husky voice reached her across the darkness.

'What?' Sian was stunned. Had she spoken her

thoughts aloud or had he developed a skill for mind reading?

His chuckle was unforgivably sly.

'You were wondering how I'd kept my boyish figure. . .'

'Boyish?' She choked as she tried to prevent the word emerging. 'A bit narcissistic at your age, don't you think?'

'It was my age that made me take it up,' he replied, ignoring the catty side of her remark. 'In our line of work we can spend long hours sitting hunched over an operating table. I decided to do something to minimise the damage.'

'I took up circuit training and swimming,' she murmured in a soft voice, the closest she dared come to an apology.

His brief burst of laughter made her jump.

'Wouldn't you know it?' His tone was tinged with bitterness and she was glad she couldn't see his face. 'We parted company nearly two years ago and we're still doing the same things, making the same decisions. . .' His voice tailed off and she knew he was remembering the time their decisions had put them at cross purposes; knew he was remembering that he had sworn never to forgive her.

Sian heard him turn over and thump his pillow and thought longingly of the nights when he had drawn her against the cradle of his body, his arm wrapped securely around her as if he would never let her go.

She squeezed her eyes tight shut and buried her face in the pillow, determined not to cry again. She had cried enough over Sam Forrester, begging him to listen to her.

Well, she wouldn't be doing any more begging. It

didn't matter what he thought of her any more because she didn't care about him. He was just another colleague with whom she would be working for a week, and then they would never see each other again.

Silently, she cursed her own stupidity as she felt the familiar pain in her heart.

'Goodnight, my love,' she whispered soundlessly, repeating the ritual which had been part of the fabric of their lives for five long years.

The dream was never very clear—for the most part, more a series of emotions than events—and she never knew when it would next strike.

Over the last two years it had gradually lessened, only coming to torment her when her spirits were low.

If she had been thinking logically, she supposed she should have expected it to return now that Sam had suddenly reappeared in her life.

All she could ever remember was that Sam was in the dream and that he wouldn't let her come near him, his anger palpable although his actual words were indecipherable as she begged him to listen.

This time was no different from the rest. She woke suddenly, her heart beating frantically and her face wet with tears, her nightdress and bedclothes twisted around her exhausted body.

Then, this time was *very* different. This time Sam was leaning over her, his naked shoulders impossibly broad in the pale grey light of dawn, his fists planted firmly on either side of her on the mattress, his dark eyes piercing her with his anger.

'I suppose it's some sort of consolation,' he said grimly, 'to know that your guilty conscience is still making you suffer for what you did.'

CHAPTER TWO

BY THE time her alarm shrilled its summons, Sam had
left the room, much to Sian's relief.

After his brief burst of venom he had returned to bed
and apparently gone straight to sleep, while Sian had
curled up around her misery.

She was desperate for another hour of sleep but was
convinced that Sam's potent bitterness had robbed her
of any likelihood of it.

In the end she had fallen so deeply asleep that the
mere act of opening her eyes was a struggle—until the
phone rang right beside her ear.

'Hello,' she mumbled, trying to switch her brain into
gear. 'Room. . .' What *was* the number of the room?

'Dr Forrester?' The mission manager's voice sounded
terrifyingly bright and alert.

'Yes?'

'I know this is very short notice, but could you
possibly come to the small conference-room before you
go down for your breakfast?' It was phrased as a request
but Sian could hear the fine ring of steel under the
pleasant tone.

'Certainly,' she confirmed, all drowsiness banished.
'What time?'

'Would ten minutes be convenient?'

'Of course,' she said calmly. 'I'll see you then.'

The receiver went down with an ungentle crash as
Sian leapt out of the bed, shedding her nightdress on the
way to the shower.

24

She hoped that one day she would be able to laugh at the events of the next five minutes. As her brain revved faster and faster trying to understand why she felt as if something terrible was about to happen, everything she touched seemed to have taken on a life of its own.

From the soap which leapt out of her wet hands and across the bathroom floor to her bra, half of which somehow managed to turn itself inside out so that she had to take it off and start again, nothing went right first time.

'Thank goodness I left my clothes ready last night,' she muttered, as she tried to brush her hair and put on lipstick at the same time.

She grabbed her document-case and pulled the door shut behind her before she set off at a smart pace towards the lifts.

As she knocked on the door of the conference-room she took a quick glance at her watch and breathed a sigh of relief. It was unbelievable, but she had fifteen seconds to spare.

'Come in,' the mission manager's voice invited. 'Don't stand on ceremony.'

Sian pulled the door shut behind her and paused, her eyes fixed on the formidable shape of Sam Forrester silhouetted against the heavenly blue sky outside the panoramic windows.

What was he doing here? What had he been telling the other members of the team?

As she watched, he raised his wrist to glance at his watch. Only she saw the raised eyebrow and the wry nod he accorded her.

Immediately Sian's hackles rose. What right did he have to look so superior? Just because she had still been fast asleep when he left the room. . .

'Do make yourselves comfortable. . .'

An elegant hand indicated the casually grouped chairs.

Sian sank into one gratefully, then regretted the move when she found that she was the only one sitting. In spite of the fact that she hated having to look up at both of them, standing up again was not an option, so she leant back in the chair and tucked her feet neatly to one side as if she hadn't a care in the world.

'Certain matters have come to my attention,' the manager started briskly. 'On checking our computer records after the confusion yesterday, we found out where the mix-up occurred and have established separate files for both of you, but we also found out. . .' She paused, her slight hesitation at odds with her usual impeccable decisiveness.

'That Sian and I were husband and wife?' Sam volunteered helpfully.

'*Were* being the operative word,' Sian added coldly. 'Is that a problem?'

'No.' The reply was incisive. 'Because I will not allow it to be a problem.' Her chin came up and she looked from one to the other before she continued.

'Orbis is what matters here and it is my job to make sure that the next week runs smoothly. If that means that I have to sort out a personality clash by sending one of you home, then that is what I will do—it won't be the first time.'

Without raising her voice above a conversational tone she had laid the cards on the table.

Sian and Sam glanced at each other warily at first, as if nervous of showing any reaction in front of a third person, and the silence began to stretch out uncomfortably.

'As far as I'm concerned,' Sam finally said, 'you have absolutely nothing to worry about. As you said, it's Orbis that matters most.'

'Thank you, Dr. Forrester.' She nodded and turned towards Sian. 'And you, Dr. . .'

'I think it would be easier if you called me Sian.' She smiled at the potential for continuing confusion. 'After all, we will both be here for a week.'

'Thank you. And you must both call me Celia.' She glanced down at her watch. 'I'm sorry. This meeting has left you with very little time to eat. I will make sure the bus waits for you—it might be a long time before your next meal!'

Her Orbis wings gleamed on the lapel of her blazer as she turned to walk smartly out of the room, leaving a deep silence behind her.

'Shall we. . .?'

'Do you. . .?'

They both started to speak at once, and Sam rolled his eyes upwards and laughed wryly.

'That's another thing we still seem fated to do.'

'I was only going to say——' Sian kept her voice steady with an effort as Sam's easygoing smile reminded her of all they had lost '—shall we go down to breakfast? We can continue the discussion in the dining-room, if you think there's anything more to say.'

The smile disappeared from his face as if it had never existed.

'By all means.' He swept one hand out in an exaggerated invitation for her to precede him through the door. 'But I would like to know if you really agreed with what Celia said.'

'What, in particular?' Her throat constricted on the words as he took her elbow to usher her into the lift.

Even through the lightweight fabric of her sleeve she could feel the warmth and strength of his hand.

'Well, you never actually said whether you thought there would be a problem if you have to work with me for a week, especially as you won't be able to disappear off to your room to escape my presence.'

He took her arm again to lead her through to an empty table, and pulled the chair out for her.

'I don't anticipate any problem,' she confirmed, when her voice was once more under her control. How could he still have such an effect on her with just a polite hand at her elbow, for heaven's sake? 'It is the job we're here for which must come first.'

'Of course. How could I have forgotten?' His low voice came out flat and harsh. 'The job always comes first,' and he fixed her with dark eyes that radiated a searing mixture of ice and fire.

It was the sheer number of bodies which struck Sian most forcibly when they arrived at the hospital that morning.

A reception area which could have held up to fifty people in comfort was crammed with what looked like ten times that number.

The air-conditioning had never been intended to cope with such a situation and was failing miserably, even with the addition of auxiliary fans.

'I am so sorry for all this,' one of the host doctors apologised. 'We had organised for a number of patients to be ready for you, but many of these have arrived out of nowhere. They have heard about your visit from the media or from their families. Some have been brought here by their doctors, who remember your first visit to Beijing in 1985.

'Many of these people believe Orbis is their only hope for a miracle, and so they come. . .' He shrugged fatalistically as he indicated the crush of bodies.

'How can we possibly see all these people?' Sian murmured faintly, daunted by the overwhelming task.

'We have started already to put people into different categories and we have given them a coloured card and a number to go with their case-notes.'

As he explained the rough system which had been adopted to cope with the unprecedented numbers, the visiting faculty began to see how it would work.

'It's still going to be a hellish day's work,' Philip muttered in an aside.

'And even worse for the poor souls waiting our here in the heat,' Sian added. 'At least we'll be seeing them one at a time in our separate areas.'

Each of the visiting ophthalmologists was taken courteously to his or her temporary department, where they were introduced through interpreters to a group of host doctors specialising in their particular field.

Sian was lucky that the majority of her group was reasonably fluent in everyday English, apart from the few who understood French better, but she was grateful that the young woman who was to interpret had checked the particular terminology she would be needing.

The next three hours were a refined form of torture as Sian saw children ranging in age from two years to thirteen.

Many of them had eye diseases which also existed in her own hospital in England, but she had never seen so many of such severity—so many which could have been treated successfully if only they could have been seen earlier.

Some of the conditions she had only seen in textbooks. Others were caused by the particular dietary situation in this region of China.

As always, it was the children themselves who affected Sian the most: the little ones whose poor sight had made them stoic and patient before their time; the young teenagers who never smiled because life had shown them little to smile about.

In the midst of mayhem Sian kept working, keeping up a running commentary which interspersed gentle words to calm her patients with highly technical discussions of examination techniques and diagnosis, pathology and treatment alternatives with the host doctors.

'Sian,' a familiar voice called to her, as she was directing one of the host doctors to examine a five-year-old girl's eye through the ophthalmic microscope. She held up one hand to indicate she had heard Sam call, and continued to explain to the young doctor the significance of what he was seeing, and also what he would soon be able to do about it.

'Sorry to keep you waiting.' She finally made her way to where Sam was leaning patiently against the doorframe. 'That young doctor has the makings of a first-rate diagnostician. I was just putting in my bid for him to specialise in paediatrics!'

She smiled broadly up at him, her flat-soled shoes giving him nearly eight inches of height over her as he ushered her along the corridor towards a makeshift overflow canteen.

'I thought you were looking particularly pleased with yourself.' He returned the smile easily.

'Oh, Sam!' she breathed, a spring in her step in spite of the gruelling schedule. 'It's a fantastic feeling, knowing that what you're doing matters so much.'

'And you think it doesn't matter back home?' he said provokingly.

'Of course it does, to each individual patient, but here——' she drew in a deep breath '—I might only operate on a handful of cases over the next week, but with all those doctors watching and learning, that handful is like pebbles dropped into water—the ripples will keep spreading with each of my audience who goes back to his own hospital and starts treating more patients.'

'You're preaching to the converted,' he reminded her wryly. 'I first thought about applying to join the faculty nearly two years ago. . .' His words died, leaving an ominous silence which Sian hurried to fill.

'I applied soon after I saw a television documentary about the organisation.' She paused as they entered the crowded canteen, then, when she realised that the volume of sound would make it nearly impossible for her words to be overheard, found the courage to speak.

'Sam.' Her voice was strained. 'I realise that my name only came up for this trip because it got mixed up with yours. . .'

'Go on,' he invited, his expression very intent as he leant closer to hear her voice.

'Well, I thought perhaps you would prefer it if I was to go home so that we didn't have to see. . .'

'Don't be daft, woman. What would happen to all your patients?'

'No one has been finally chosen yet, so. . .'

'Don't you *dare* try to duck out of this!' he hissed furiously. 'Those patients need your skill and the doctors need to watch you to learn what to do.'

'I *know* that,' she whispered, equally forcefully. 'But this is a high-pressure situation and neither of us is going to be able to do our best for our patients if we're permanently having to watch what we say to each other.'

Out of the corner of her eye she saw the young doctor who had so impressed her start to walk towards them, then politely change his mind when he saw the fierce nature of their conversation.

She ran her fingers through her hair and blew out a frustrated puff of air.

'This is hardly the place to hold such a——'

'You're right,' Sam suddenly interrupted her. 'We told Celia there wouldn't be a problem if we both stayed on, so the only thing I can suggest is a truce.'

'A truce?' Sian's voice was doubtful, but it was an intriguing idea. 'How do you envisage it working?'

'I suggest that for the duration of our stay we pretend that we have never been anything more than colleagues.'

'That might be a little difficult, considering we'll be thrown together all day and we're sharing a room at night. It might be more realistic to declare a moratorium on sly digs and sarcasm. . .'

'You could be right.' He smiled ruefully, the corners of his mouth lifting in the slightly crooked grin she had thought she would never see again.

In spite of the intensity of their discussion they had both managed to finish eating just as a general exodus started.

'Round two,' Sam quipped as he escorted Sian through the milling crowd. 'Do you think you'll be able to choose suitable cases for demonstration purposes by four o'clock? Apparently the hospital staff need to know by then so that they can instruct tomorrow's patients on basic pre-op procedure.'

'Finding examples of classic cases isn't the problem. It's playing God that's getting to me.' Her throat tightened as she thought of the sad little faces which had been confronting her all morning.

'Keep your chin up,' he advised softly, as they reached the doorway to her designated area. 'Don't think of them as your patients, just try to see them as teaching opportunities.'

'Ha!' Sian scoffed. 'Try telling yourself that when you next have a two-year-old with cataracts sitting in front of you!'

'I've tried,' he admitted. 'It's bad enough when they're elderly. . .' He squeezed her shoulder gently, then walked further along the corridor and disappeared.

When the buses arrived back at the hotel late that afternoon the whole staff was subdued.

Partly, it was sheer exhaustion from the heat and the pace they had been forced to adopt, but they were all willing to admit that a large amount of their sadness was the realisation of the scale of the problem.

'Thirty million people in the world whose blindness could be cured or prevented if only they had access to the knowledge and the skill. . .' the staff nurse-anaesthetist was explaining to his volunteer opposite number as they made their way towards the lifts.

Sian was desperate for a long cool shower, but delayed her rush for the bathroom long enough to have a quick word with the audio-visual technician.

'Gavin, I'm first on in the morning and——'

'You've got nothing to worry about,' he interrupted with a grin. 'I've done lots of these operations and I promise you they're easy!'

After a startled silence, Sian suddenly realised she was having her leg pulled by a master of the art.

'You idiot!' She thumped his arm.

'I'll let you into a trade secret.' He lowered his voice as he leant towards her. 'I can arrange to remove all your wobbly bits. . .!'

Sian burst out laughing.

'All right,' she conceded. 'I can take a hint!'

'Honestly, Sian, you'll be fine. Don't worry about it or you'll end up in a worse state than ever. I see it all the time.' They walked to the lifts together and joined several other members of the team on their way up.

Sian had reached the door to her room before she realised that she hadn't got her key with her.

She slumped tiredly against the wall, contemplating the trek back down to the reception desk, when she remembered that she hadn't handed the key in on her way out to the bus this morning.

Casting her mind back over the frantic events of the first quarter of an hour of her day, she was convinced that she must have left the key on the dressing-table in her hurry to get to the conference-room on time.

'Oh, what an idiot!' she muttered, as she took a deep breath and knocked on the door.

Silence.

'Don't tell me he's still downstairs somewhere,' she moaned, giving the door another hard rap.

'All right. All right.' The deep rumble of Sam's voice reached her just before he opened the door.

Sian was struck speechless by the sight which met her eyes.

Sam had obviously been in the shower when she knocked. His body was shimmering under the lighting in the hallway, with rivulets of water trickling over the smooth swells of his shoulders and chest and down his taut belly until they met the precarious cover of a hastily donned towel.

'Don't you think this is taking the strangers bit just a little too far?' he queried sarcastically, raking the fingers of one hand through the thick wet strands of hair plastered darkly to his forehead.

'Wh-what?' she stumbled, her brain still overloaded by his potent nearness.

'I said,' he enunciated slowly, as if she was simple-minded, 'don't you think this is going too far — knocking before you come in the room as if we were strangers?'

'It would be, if that was why I knocked,' Sian replied tartly, as she strode past him to pick her key up from its resting place on the dressing-table. 'As it was, with this inside the room, it was a little difficult to open the door without assistance.'

She dropped the key back down with a clatter, and sank gratefully on to the side of her bed to ease her feet out of her shoes as she ran her fingers through the slightly limp curls clustered around the back of her neck.

The continuing silence had her raising her eyes to find Sam leaning back against the door with his arms folded across the intimidating width of his chest. He was contemplating her with a look of anguish on his face which nearly stopped her heart.

'Sam?' she whispered. 'What is it? What's the matter?'

'Why did you do it?' he said, his husky voice filled with sadness. 'Why did you cut your hair?'

'My. . .' Involuntarily her hand went up as if to touch the tousled strands, as she remembered how her hair had been when they had known each other before.

The dark strands had flowed in a silky river right down to her waist, and Sam had revelled in arranging the shiny profusion to cover her body and his when they wore nothing else.

Many times he had whispered how it felt to him that she kept her hair bound at work, only releasing its beauty in his presence.

As she watched his expression, she saw the grief which mirrored her own memories and was filled again by the bitter desolation which had overcome her when she had taken the scissors to her hair herself.

In that moment she had known the overwhelming emotion which could cause some women to sacrifice themselves on their husbands' graves. She had felt so utterly empty—as if, having lost Sam, she had no right to be attractive to any other man.

It was only later, when her emotions had returned to a more even keel, that the anger had come, the anger which had burned fiercely enough to fuel her determination to get her career back on track again in spite of him.

'I. . . It's more convenient to have it like this,' she murmured weakly, not daring to meet his eyes for fear he would see the real reason.

'Convenient!' he sneered, shrugging away from the door and striding barefoot back towards his interrupted shower. 'You seem to set such great store by convenience. What will you do if you have to wing it—if you have to put up with a less than convenient situation——?'

'Now, just you wait a minute. . .'

She might as well have saved her breath, as he didn't even acknowledge her interruption.

'Do you still put your own selfish needs first?' he demanded, every word an accusation. 'Have you learnt anything in the last two years or are you still as destructive as ever?' His dark eyes shredded her coldly.

Sian's control shattered with the violence of her hurt.

'How dare you?' she shrieked, as her heart contracted in agony, and she flew at him with her hands curved like the talons of a bird of prey.

Sam side-stepped her fury easily, trapping her wrists before she came near enough to rake his smooth naked flesh with her nails.

'Hardly very original,' he mocked, as he pulled her arms behind her back to trap both in one powerful hand. 'I believe our hosts have a saying which translates as "He who strikes the first blow has lost the argument". . .'

His free hand circled her shoulders to pull her towards him, preventing her from continuing her vicious intentions at closer range.

As she came in contact with the furnace-heat of Sam's bare flesh, all her breath left her lungs, taking with it any inclination to fight.

Her nose was pressed against his chest, her eyes almost on a level with the pulse throbbing at the base of his throat.

'Now, then. . .' as if from a long way away she heard his deep voice rumble from the depths of his chest, and followed the sound with her eyes until she was watching his mouth moving to form words.

His lips.

She had cried when she had remembered the unimaginable pleasure they had brought her, and her heart had broken anew each time she remembered that it would never happen again.

'Sian?'

He had released her hands and was holding her by her arms, shaking her gently to attract her attention.

'What?' Her eyes moved slowly from their contemplation of his mouth, upwards until they met the glinting mystery of his own dark gaze.

'Dammit, Sian,' he muttered huskily, his grasp softening still further until it became a sensuous caress as his palms circled the rounded shape of her shoulders, sliding the silky fabric of her shirt over her skin. 'Don't look at me like that. . .' His voice was becoming deeper, rougher.

'Don't. . .?'

She couldn't concentrate on his words, couldn't drag her eyes away from the heat building in his dark depths until it seemed as if it would consume her.

'Sian. . .' he groaned, as his mouth swooped to capture her own in a devastating conflagration.

Time ceased to exist as they stood locked in each other's arms, and Sian discovered that she had forgotten nothing of the delight she and Sam could bring to each other.

Sam.

From the first time she had met him there had been no one else. He had been the other half of her soul—the one person in the whole world she would trust with her life, with her heart.

And he had broken it.

'No-o.' She turned her head away, wrenching their mouths apart. 'No, Sam.' She shook her head violently, her whole body trembling with the effort of separating herself from the only person she had ever loved.

Sian had made certain she stayed out of Sam's way while they freshened themselves after a hard day, but she needn't have worried. He seemed just as keen to avoid her, the atmosphere in their room frigid enough to need a fire to thaw it out, in spite of the heat of the day.

When she arrived in the small conference-room, slightly early for the meeting, she had seated herself between Philip and Joan, the head nurse.

The two of them had worked together before in Hyderabad in India, when Philip had been on his first stint with Orbis, and kept Sian laughing with the tales of some of the problems they'd had on the old DC-8 which had recently gone into honourable retirement.

'She was worked hard from 1982 until 1994, but when she started having power-supply failure it was time she was replaced,' Joan explained.

'She was bad enough when the power was working,' Philip complained ironically.

'Especially the air-conditioning when you're stuck in a bunny suit,' Joan agreed, and they both laughed at Sian's expression.

'You'll find out all about it tomorrow,' they warned, just as the meeting was called to order.

Sian couldn't help herself glancing quickly around the small conference-room. For a moment she was unable to see Sam, until suddenly the dark-haired man seated almost directly opposite her in the loosely gathered circle raised his head to fix her with a fierce stare.

Her heart gave an unexpected lurch before it settled into a slightly faster beat, and she was conscious that her cheeks had become warmer as she concentrated on avoiding his gaze.

'Right now, ladies and gentlemen.' The mission manager called them to attention.

'How does Celia manage to look immaculate twenty-four hours a day?' Sian muttered in an aside to Joan.

'No idea,' she whispered. 'In over a year I've never seen her with so much as a hair out of place—and she's still a likeable person!' She pulled a face and tugged her skirt mock-primly over her knees with a twinkle in her eyes.

'Before you get down to the main work of the evening,' Celia continued, referring to a brief note in her hand, 'it will be a seven-thirty departure tomorrow morning. The host surgeons who will be assisting will arrive at eight-thirty and the first patients at nine.'

She glanced up at the door as a late-comer slid in quietly, then nodded at his silent apology.

'As you may know, there is now an accord between Orbis and China, specifying that we will hold three training programmes in China every year. On the first trip Orbis made to Beijing ten years ago, only ten per cent of the Chinese doctors who attended the programme were using the operating microscope. Four years later, as a result of Orbis's training, eighty per cent were performing microsurgery routinely. . .'

In spite of her determination, Sian found that her attention had wandered, as had her eyes, which were now fixed on a certain dark-haired man on the other side of the group.

His expression was so familiar to her, as endearing as an earnest child's as he concentrated with his usual intensity on what Celia was saying.

Sian had often whiled away her time watching Sam's expressions as he studied or while he was working. He had a knack for blocking out extraneous distractions, which she had delighted in testing to destruction. . .

'Sian, here——' Celia's use of her name drew her sharply back to the present '—will be operating on a two-year-old with a severe squint.' She smiled across at

Sian as she spoke. 'As the paediatric specialist on board this week, she will be first in the firing line each day, as we always take the children first on the list.

'Tomorrow morning,' she continued, referring briefly to her note, 'we are expecting all fifty seats on board to be filled, as well as the second classroom in one of the hangars with a further two hundred seats.'

She had known before she came out to join Orbis that these numbers could be expected, but Sian still felt her stomach clench with nervous tension at the thought of the responsibility.

Not that she doubted her ability to operate successfully on her little patient; that was the least of her worries. It was the uniqueness of the whole situation which was causing her palms to become damp and her shoulders to tighten.

It was the importance of presenting the method in such a way that her audience would be able to re-create her results once they returned to their own hospitals.

'Those of you who have been on Orbis before will notice the refinements which have been built into the DC-10. I expect the old hands will take great delight in telling the first-timers what they had to put up with in the old DC-8. . .!'

Sian joined in the general laughter, as this was exactly what had already been happening.

'The first trip to Beijing in the DC-10 took place in July last year—in fact it was the first trip since she became the "new" Orbis. Hopefully, we will be using her for the next fifteen years and you will all have other chances to work on her in that time.'

The medical director took the floor then, and a rapid discussion took place in which the various videotapes and slide presentations available were slotted into a tentative timetable. These would be shown to the visiting doctors over the sophisticated audio-visual equipment, while patients were being prepared for surgery or between the various surgical cases during the day.

'As usual, the fellows will be taking charge of the laser work. We should be able to cover a wide range of laser techniques each day, just as we've timetabled the five patients for tomorrow. Our hosts have asked particularly that we demonstrate the treatment of detached retina and corneal clouding subsequent to cataract removal.' He glanced across at Sam.

'I understand you will be giving the slide lecture on retinal detachment tomorrow morning?'

'That's right.' Sam smiled as he ran the fingers of one hand through his hair.

He's nervous, Sian realised suddenly, remembering the tell-tale gesture of old. Big, strong Sam Forrester, the ophthalmologist with nerves of steel and a poker face, was actually showing signs of nervousness.

There was no time to ponder the significance of her discovery because the medical director was still speaking.

'Sam will be delivering his preliminary lecture while your first patient is being prepped.' He had turned so that he was speaking to her directly, but the explanation was for all of them.

'Meanwhile, as soon as you are told that your patient is ready, you'll go back and change, then you and your assistant will come forward for your five minutes at the scrub-sink. There's a window between the scrub-room and OR so that you can see when the gurney is in position.

'When you're all gloved and glowned, the audio-visual department will give the signal "ready to go live", and the lecture will be stopped for live transmission of the surgery.'

He looked around the circle and smiled. 'That's pretty much what will be happening for the rest of the week, give or take a hiccup. Any questions so far?'

'About the host ophthalmologists?' Philip queried. 'The ones who are having the hands-on experience?'

'With the larger operating-room on the DC-10, things are working really smoothly. There'll still be two local nurses in OR shadowing our own, plus the nurse-anaesthetist, as well as the visiting surgeon and host ophthalmologist. The air-conditioning is much more efficient than on the DC-8 but it can still get pretty warm with all those bodies in there!'

'Having said that, the host doctors are usually the cream of the crop and so keen to learn that they're a pleasure to work with.'

'At least we'll all be getting a free sauna,' quipped one of the nurses, causing a heartfelt groan. 'Well, it means we don't have to worry so much about all the gorgeous food at the official events. We can sweat it all off!'

'Speaking of official events——' Celia raised her hand for attention and received a groan of her own '—the host doctors have invited us to a reception tomorrow night at eight. There will probably be several representatives of the Chinese Ministry of Health. As you probably know, they have been responsible for providing the co-ordination and major support for the Orbis programmes in China.'

'How many of the team are invited?' Gavin queried.

'Everyone,' Celia confirmed simply. 'That includes any wives or husbands who have travelled with you, even though they aren't team members. Our hosts are laying on some traditional Chinese entertainment.'

'How late do you anticipate this going on?' Sam's deep voice enquired quietly. 'We'll have had a gruelling day and we have to be up again the next morning.' His eyes brushed over Sian, and she felt the impact like the flickering of a flame over her skin and shivered in reaction.

'Our hosts realise that, and have promised that it won't go on too late. They are providing transport each way, so everyone can relax. There will probably be a couple more events before the end of the week, but we might be able to arrange it so that half of the team goes each time, to leave the other half with some free time. I'll let you know the details as soon as I get them.'

'What about dress code?' Sian asked.

'Good point,' Celia agreed. 'The men can wear a suit or a staff blazer. The ladies will probably fit in much better with our hosts if they wear something like a cocktail dress.' She glanced down at her watch before looking around the circle once more.

'If there are no more questions, we're all free until breakfast tomorrow. Don't forget, I'm here if there are any problems that need sorting out.'

Sian smiled as she watched her colleagues preparing to leave the small conference-room. Their reaction reminded her of schoolchildren at the end of the day's lessons.

Her face was still softened by a reminiscent smile when she felt the tingle which told her she was being watched.

Her eyes swung around the milling bodies to encounter Sam's long muscular body sprawled like a lazy lion's in his chair, his dark eyes fixed speculatively on her. His

dark brows were drawn slightly together as though he
was trying to solve a puzzle.

She caught his eye and raised one of her own
eyebrows questioningly at him.

For several long seconds their gazes meshed and the
sights and sounds of the rest of the room faded into
obscurity.

It was as if they were both holding their breath and
waiting for something momentous to happen.

'Sam?'

Philip's friendly voice intruded with the impact of a
hand-grenade and they were both shocked into
awareness.

'Are you going to join us for a drink in the bar? You,
too, Sian?'

Sian shook her head, momentarily bereft of speech.

'No, thanks, Philip.' Sam's voice sounded slightly
husky. 'I'm first up tomorrow. You've done this before,
but it's still a bit nerve-racking for us novices, until we
get into the swing of it.'

'OK. See you in the morning,' he said cheerily as he
left the room.

Silence descended again, and this time the threads of
tension which ran through it had grown stronger and
more numerous until Sian began to feel as though she
was becoming surrounded by a net.

Sam cleared his throat and drew himself out of his
chair and straightened up.

'I'm ready to go to sleep.' His voice was a distorted
rumble as he stretched both arms up to their full extent.

From her position, still seated in her chair, Sian saw
Sam's shirt pull away from the waistband of his trousers
and was treated to a view of the taut tanned stomach
bisected vertically by a dark line of hair.

She was riveted by the sight, knowing from her recent encounters that, just as she remembered all too vividly, that dark stripe still widened out into a broad wedge as it travelled upwards towards the tawny discs of his flat male nipples. The dark silky furring on his chest was just visible as a shadow through his pale shirt as it stretched over the impressive muscles of his chest.

He stooped forward suddenly to retrieve the small leather-bound notebook from the floor beside his chair.

'Are you coming to bed, then?' he said calmly, as he turned towards the door.

CHAPTER THREE

THE first thing Sian thought about when the alarm woke her the next morning was Sam's calm voice asking her if she was coming to bed.

'Wh-what!' she had squeaked, as breathless as if she'd hit a brick wall, while her pulse-rate had doubled. 'I'm s-sorry,' she had stumbled, frantically trying to find the words in a memory suddenly gone blank. 'Did you say. . .?'

'It's late.' Sam had thrown the words calmly over his shoulder without slowing his progress across the room. 'If we're going to get enough sleep tonight, we ought to go to bed now.'

He finally paused by the door and reached one hand out to rest on the wall by the light switch before turning back partially towards her to see if she was following.

'Sian?' His eyebrows had drawn into a deep V as he had seen that she was still sitting in her chair. 'What's the matter? Didn't you hear what I suggested?'

It had been like a revelation; like a bolt of lightning striking on a clear day.

'Yes, Sam,' she had hissed through gritted teeth. '*I* heard what you suggested, but I don't think *you* did.'

There had been such a deathly silence between them that Sian could almost have sworn that she could hear Sam's brain replaying his words.

She knew as soon as he realised what he'd said by the dark tide of colour which flooded across his leanly sculpted cheekbones.

Almost immediately his eyes flashed an angry look at her.

'You know what I meant,' he growled, before his mouth closed into a grim line.

'*I* know what you meant,' Sian heard herself murmuring softly, before she added slyly, 'I wonder if *you* know what you meant? It sounded like quite a Freudian slip. . .!'

She sailed blithely past him and out into the corridor, delighted to have had the last word.

As she made her way to the lift she was conscious of his eyes burning into her back, but daren't glance back even for the briefest look to see if it was her imagination.

Finally, she reached the lift and stepped through the open doors, pressing the button to her floor before she allowed herself to lean back against the panelled wall— just in time to watch the doors close in front of Sam's face.

All the way up to her floor she was conscious of the tremble in her legs and was grateful that she was alone as she held on to the ornate rail which circled the lift.

She was torn between collapsing on the floor with relief that she had escaped unscathed, and bursting into laughter at the expression on Sam's face when she made no attempt to hold the lift for him.

In the event, she had seized the opportunity to use the bathroom first, taking a wicked delight in shampooing her hair at her leisure, then wallowing in a deep bath of scented bubbles until she felt almost boneless.

Part of the joy in taking so long in the bathroom was lost when she finally emerged to an empty room, and Sian finally had to admit to herself that deep inside she had been looking forward to a confrontation with Sam.

Disgruntled, she flounced into bed but, despite her determination to wait until Sam arrived, her eyes began to grow heavy and she knew no more.

Breakfast-time arrived far too quickly for Sian. There was little room in her stomach for anything other than the butterflies but, knowing that her next meal might be a long time away, she forced herself to eat a sensible amount. It would do no one any good if she was too hungry to concentrate or, even worse, if she fainted due to low blood-sugar.

Gavin sat beside her on the trip out to the airport and tried to get her talking—without much success.

'Oh, dear——' he tried teasing '—I'm really going to earn my money trying to salvage enough tape between your wobbly bits to show those poor doctors! Perhaps they'd prefer it if I filmed a guided tour of Orbis?'

'Oh, Gavin, I'm sorry,' Sian apologised. 'I promise you I'll be all right as soon as we get started, but this is the most nerve-racking thing I've ever done. Things don't usually get to me like this. I feel such a fool. No one would believe I'm a fully qualified——'

'What about your first date?' he challenged suddenly.

'What?' She sat back, open-mouthed at the question.

'Well, are you more scared now than the first time you went out on a date?'

'No. Yes. Oh, it's completely different!' she objected with a startled chuckle.

'What about the first time you drove a car?' This time the voice came from behind her—the nurse-anaesthetist.

'Or the first time you stood under the mistletoe?' one of the nurses chipped in.

Sian couldn't help laughing.

'All right, all right. Stop! This could start getting into dangerous waters. . .' Her voice trailed off as she met Sam's eyes for the first time that morning and, without a word being spoken, she knew he was thinking of the first time *they* had kissed, the first time they. . .

'There's Orbis!' several voices called simultaneously, and the connection between them was broken.

Orbis drew their eyes like a magnet, her white and navy livery gleaming brightly in the sunlight with the logo proudly displayed on the tail.

'She's beautiful,' Sian whispered as they drove close. 'And so big. . .'

It was easy to tell which were the first-time members of the team—they were the ones standing looking up at Orbis as they took in the sight of her for the first time.

The rest of the team were scurrying around performing their allotted tasks. The steps were positioned against the side of the plane at the same time as the massive generator was let down out of the storage area in the plane's belly and started up. It would be providing all the power for each of the many systems necessary throughout the day.

The four huge LD3 containers full of medical supplies were lowered. It would take two deliveries per mission to keep them stocked, usually flown in by friendly airlines.

As Sian made her way towards the foot of the steps she was handed an armful of packages to take up and was met at the top by Joan, who replaced her burden with disposable booties to put over her shoes as she stepped inside the back of the plane for the first time.

'A quick guided tour,' Joan decided, as the visiting faculty formed a group around her.

'Immediately to your right, at the very back of the

plane, are the toilets. To your left is the corridor which runs right down this side of the plane until you reach the class-room in what was the first-class passenger section.' She spoke crisply as she led them along the corridor.

'Behind that is the audio-visual section, then the laser and examination room. There's a small conference-room in behind that before we come to the OR.'

After a lightning whirl past an astounding array of electronic equipment in the a-v section, and the more familiar ophthalmic microscopes and lasers, she had come to rest with one finger pointing towards a bulkhead.

'For obvious reasons, there is no access to the OR from the front of the plane. All staff and patients are processed through from the back of the plane. Each patient is wheeled into the OR on a gurney, passing through the instrument-room and steriliser-room on the way. After the operation, they come back to the recovery-room towards the back of the plane.'

She led them through the recovery area, where three empty gurneys waited in a row, and pointed into the instrument-room which led directly to the steriliser-room and scrub-room, with the familiar sight of the high sloping sink and long-armed taps.

At intervals throughout the plane there were monitors which would enable the various members of staff to follow the progress of each transmission. Joan had mentioned them as they had passed, then pointed out the supplies of familiar pale blue unisex cotton scrubs while she and Sian started to get ready.

'On the old DC-8 there was a camera at the back, by the recovery area. Unfortunately for the staff,' Joan continued with a twinkle in her eyes, 'it meant that the a-v department was in a position to monitor the area while we were stripping off and getting into scrubs.'

'I should imagine that could cause a few problems as well as hilarity,' Sian suggested through her laughter.

'Yes,' Joan agreed. 'One visiting surgeon insisted on wearing Union-Jack underwear, but some of the nurses from countries with strict religious conventions found it very difficult and resorted to changing in the toilets.'

'So we're quite safe stripping off back here now?'

'Safe from the a-v peeping Toms, if not from each other,' she chuckled. 'Some of the visiting surgeons are rather gorgeous!'

Aren't they just? Sian thought, as she tucked the short-sleeved V-necked top into the matching trousers. She couldn't help remembering what Sam had looked like with droplets of water running down his chest, and clenched her hands at the remembered feel of his smooth, warm skin.

'After you've finished——' Joan's voice broke into her salacious thoughts '—if you want to go forward to the class-room, you'll need to cover up in one of these bunny suits.'

'Pardon?' Sian looked at her in amazement. 'I thought you and Gavin were pulling my leg.'

'They're a disposable all-in-one cover-up, just like the babywear—hence the name, I suppose. The only trouble is you can get very hot in them. . .'

'Joan?' One of the nurses stuck her head round the corner of the steriliser-room.

'Coming!' Joan called back, then smiled at Sian. 'See you later, OK?'

Sian smiled in return and nodded before turning away and taking stock of her surroundings while she pulled a disposable hat on over her dark curls.

A glimpse of movement out of the corner of her eye had her watching the arrival of a coach full of smartly dressed people who were welcomed and immediately led up to the class-room at the front of the plane.

The first half of her audience had arrived safely. Soon they would be having Sam's presentation while her patient was made ready.

'Excuse me, please.' The softly spoken words came from behind her, and she whirled round in surprise and saw the neatly suited gentleman standing behind her.

'Oh! Hello.' She smiled warmly as she recognised Dr Lu. 'Can I help you?'

He was the young ophthalmologist who had impressed her so much at the hospital yesterday.

'I have the honour of operating with you this day,' he said, his words awkwardly shy.

'Good!' Sian held her hand out to him in welcome. 'I'm delighted.'

He shook her hand gingerly and she was surprised to note that his hand was almost the same size as her own, the fingers slender, the nails cut very short.

'First you will need to get into scrubs,' she said, glancing at her watch before she slipped it off and put it away with her clothes.

'Please?'

'How much English do you understand?' she demanded bluntly, suddenly realising just how difficult it would be to have an assistant who wouldn't be able to react fast enough because he had to wait for a translation of her request. With anything up to ten nationalities on board Orbis at a time this must be an ongoing problem.

'I understand more than I speak.' He smiled ruefully.

'But some words are not taught in school to have the same meaning.'

'Ah.' She nodded. 'So if I said you need to change your clothes. . .?'

'Then, I would have asked for some. . .scrubs?' He grinned mischievously.

'Right!' Sian handed him a neat pile and directed him out of the traffic lane as several other people arrived in a group.

The latest arrivals were just completing their change when the monitors burst into technicolor life, causing one young Chinese nurse to squeal when Sam's voice spoke right behind her.

The next fifteen minutes were a bittersweet time for Sian as she watched Sam's presentation, marvelling again at how clearly he was able to present his material and how patient he was as his listeners' words were translated when they questioned him.

Her concentration was broken by a hand grasping her elbow.

'Your patient has arrived,' Joan murmured in her ear, and Sian followed her through.

The solemn little mite was clinging fearfully to her mother's neck. She had a large label pinned to her dress, as would each of their patients, detailing the condition for which they were being operated.

In this child's case the problem was obvious, as one eye turned severely towards her nose.

Sian reached out to run the backs of her fingers over the child's petal-soft skin, and screwed her nose up at her. Immediately, she was rewarded with a cheeky grin.

'You're going to be a real little beauty,' Sian murmured, as she tapped the little nose with the tip of one finger.

Sam's voice was still all around her as he continued with his talk, and she was struck suddenly with a deep feeling of loss. She and Sam could have had a child by now. . .

She brought herself up sharply. This was neither the time nor the place for might-have-beens.

Within a few minutes, an intravenous line had been set up, and Sian had demonstrated to Dr Lu the method for measuring the minute cuts she would make in the muscles controlling the eye to correct the squint.

'She will be under general anaesthetic for the oper-ation,' Sian explained, as she completed her tests. 'We do this for all the children as it is easier for us and less frightening for them, especially if they have a long operation.'

'And for the adults?' Dr Lu questioned.

'They have a local anaesthetic and are conscious during the operation.'

'Have you ever tried operating on a patient under acupuncture?' Dr Lu challenged quietly, the glint in his eyes not quite hidden.

'Have you?' She turned the question back on him.

'Only once,' he admitted with a smile. 'So far!'

'And?'

'I was. . .pleasantly surprised.' He enunciated the words carefully. 'The patient was very calm and the recovery time was much faster even than under a local anaesthetic.'

'Perhaps this is something which the West needs to learn more about—a real exchange of information.' She thought for a moment. 'Would there be any possibility of observing an operation under acupuncture at the hospital while we're here?'

'I will ask if this is possible.'

Sian caught the 'patient ready' signal out of the corner of her eye and led the way into the scrub-room, where they each performed the meticulous cleaning routine before they donned mask and gown and were assisted into gloves.

Dr Lu had been watching through the round port-hole window into the OR.

'The patient has been wheeled through,' he said, just as Sian was having large clear plastic bags slipped over her sterile gloves.

'I'll take them off after I've positioned the equipment,' she explained when she saw his questioning look, and she pushed her way through to the operating-room.

Her little patient was almost invisible under the cloths draped over her. One eye was visible through the opening, the eyelids held open and the eye itself immobilised chemically.

Sian settled herself at the head of the table and reached up to move the operating microscope into position. She knew that the 'ready to go live' message had been passed to Sam when his talk ended abruptly. From now on, what she could see through the micro-scope was being picked up and relayed to the monitors on board and in the secondary class-room across the tarmac.

'Good-morning.' Sian paused to swallow nervously. 'My name is Dr Sian Forrester and my colleague is Dr Lu. Our patient is two and a half years old and has lateral strabismus.'

'Good-morning.' The medical director's voice sounded clear and close as he took up the initial commentary.

'This patient has undergone a complete battery of tests to evaluate her eyes. There was no evidence of neurological disease, and ultrasound examination showed that all the structures of her eye appear normal and healthy.'

As Sian held her hands out for the plastic bags to be removed, she heard the medical directors detailing the administration of local anaesthetic into the facial nerve to prevent the eyelid from trying to blink, and into the nerves controlling the eyeball itself.

The instrument tray was swung out into position and Sian held her hand out for the scalpel.

As the instrument appeared in the field of view it seemed enormous, as did the fine tremor of the gloved hand holding it. She paused briefly and drew in a deep breath, and let it out in a silent stream while she allowed the tension to drain out of her shoulders.

After that, the surgery went as smoothly as if she was in her own hospital back in England, the OR nurses and nurse-anaesthetist performing their tasks with practised efficiency even as they were demonstrating their work to their host shadows.

Sian found herself slipping into a comfortable routine, detailing simply and clearly what she was doing as she was doing it, and explaining the reasons why.

'The medial rectus muscle was pulling the eye in towards the nose. Now that this has been repositioned, we are shortening the lateral rectus muscle so that it will pull the eye further outwards so that the eye will be straight.'

She paused for a moment to close her eyes and gather her concentration for the final stages.

A stray thought popped into her head.

This was the first time that Sam had observed her operating since they had finished their training. Once they were both qualified, they had both been too busy seeing their own patients to have time to observe each other, even though she had always admired Sam's technique.

She opened her eyes again and focused on the eye exposed in front of her, a lingering sadness like a soft grey shadow round her heart.

The final touch in the procedure was the insertion, to hold the muscles in place, of special adjustable sutures which were left with long threads.

'These long threads are left deliberately in case the eye is not perfectly straight after surgery. They will enable us to do any fine tuning without the patient having to undergo further surgery.'

Dr Lu took over the placement of the second set of sutures, his work as meticulous as Sian had anticipated.

'What is the success rate for this operation?' The medical director relayed the question through to the OR.

'With these adjustable sutures, the actual operation to straighten the eye is virtually one hundred per cent successful,' Sian answered.

'As far as the preservation of binocular vision is concerned, the sooner the correction can be made, the less chance there is that the weak eye will give up functioning. This, of course, is why it is important for young children's eyesight to be checked from birth. That way, any problems can be caught as soon as they occur and there is a better chance that their sight can be saved.'

Sian straightened up from her slightly hunched position, as a protective patch was taped into position over the eye, and rotated her stiff shoulders.

'Thank you, Dr Lu.' She smiled tiredly, amazed at how exhausted she felt after just one operation.

'No, I thank *you* for the honour of assisting you.' He gave a little bow, his dark eyes very serious over the edge of his mask as they turned to leave the OR.

Joan appeared at his elbow.

'If you'd like to take off your mask, hat and booties, Dr Lu, you can go forward to the class-room to join the other doctors.' She held out her hand to receive the small pile of disposable blue paper objects, and received his polite thanks in return.

Sian followed them through to the recovery area and listened while he spoke to the little girl's mother. Although she couldn't understand a single word either of them said, a translation wasn't necessary. Her happy tears were enough.

As she watched him turn to walk along the corridor towards the class-room, she saw a row of little faces at the door of the plane, their eyes huge with amazement.

'Who are our friends?' She indicated their junior audience with her hand.

'Oh, that often happens.' Joan smiled. 'It doesn't matter what country we go to, they're all fascinated by the plane. It doesn't take long before they get up the courage to dare each other to climb the steps. Once they get that far and realise they won't be chased away as long as they stay outside, we end up with a semi-permanent population around the door.'

Sian checked her little patient again, then put on a bunny suit to go forward to watch the end of Sam's presentation, then remained to see Philip's first operation on the monitor. She was amazed at the superb quality of the pictures, and realised all over again how innovative the concept of Orbis had been.

She was surrounded by ophthalmic surgeons who would never have had the chance to assist in operations of this type if it weren't for the advent of such a mobile specialist unit.

At midday, the ambulance arrived to take the patients whose operations had been completed to the local hospital.

'They'll be back later on this afternoon to take the next group of patients away,' Joan confirmed. 'The fellows will go in tomorrow with the host doctors to check that everything has gone well, then, depending on the type of operation they've had, they go home after one or two days.'

'What happens about follow-up care?'

'They decide that between them when they examine the patient.'

'Joan. . .?' a voice called from the instrument-room.

'Coming. . .' She paused briefly to check the time on the digital display. 'Lunch should be here any minute,' she advised before she sped away.

A few minutes later there was a general exodus of staff, leaving just a skeleton crew on board. The rest congregated in the shade under the plane, donning earplugs against the constant roar of the generator.

'Wouldn't it be cooler to eat on the plane?' Sian enquired, straining to make herself heard as she fanned herself with a paperback book. 'There's air-conditioning inside and it would be so much quieter.'

'It's a lovely thought, but no one's allowed to take any food on board. Otherwise we'd all be in there!'

Sian gazed out across the tarmac, almost mesmerised by the shimmer of the heat haze. At intervals through-out the morning she had been vaguely aware of the take-offs and landings of other planes, but Orbis had been carefully positioned—far enough out of the way not to disrupt the normal efficiency of the airport without leaving too much distance for personnel and supplies to travel.

Under the belly of the plane there was plenty of room for everyone to relax in the shade, grateful for the fitful breeze while they made half-hearted attempts at conversation over the unavoidable noise.

Sian felt a prickle of awareness run up the back of her neck just before Sam's long legs halted beside her. She looked up from her cross-legged position at his feet, her eyes travelling slowly up the long, lean length of his body. He still looked completely cool and composed in spite of the fact that she knew he had been nervous about his presentation this morning.

Finally she reached the shadowed enigma of his face, partially obscured by sunglasses.

She intercepted a strange half-smile which flickered fleetingly around his mouth, but was unable to see whether it touched his eyes.

'Congratulations,' he said flatly, his familiar tones easy to decipher at such close range in spite of the noise of the generator. 'Your technique seems to be better than ever.'

'Thank you.' She acknowledged the compliment warily, his austere expression making her uncomfortably certain that there was more to come.

'Obviously you made the right choice when you decided you would rather have a successful career than take a chance on marriage and a family.' He strode away towards the group sitting further along in the shadows, leaving Sian totally speechless.

CHAPTER FOUR

SIAN was grateful that the rest of the day was frantically busy, as it left her little time to brood over what Sam had said.

On the odd occasions when his scathing words had flooded into her mind, she had ruthlessly pushed them into a small dark corner. Later, when she was alone, she would take them out and examine his painfully unfair denunciation. Perhaps, after all this time, she would be able to come to terms with his cruelty.

In the meantime, there was work to be done and she had given her word that her personal problems would not affect the mission.

Once the final operation of the day was over, the last patients had been transferred to the ambulance and taken to the local hospital.

Tomorrow they would be visited by the host doctors and the fellows from Orbis. Most would be able to go home within a day or two, returning later for stitches to be removed and progress checks.

Meanwhile, the host doctors and their translators were filing off the front of the plane with courteous expressions of thanks.

Dr Lu made a point of searching Sian out.

'We will see you this evening?' he asked politely.

'Oh, yes.' She smiled at his earnest face and couldn't help thinking that, in spite of their similarity in age, he seemed so frighteningly young. 'Thank you for asking. We will all be coming.'

'May I ask you a question?' His tone was diffident.

'Certainly.'

'Are you and the other Dr Forrester married to each other, or is this a common name in your country?'

In spite of the warning jolt of surprise at his question, Sian was quietly amused to see the hint of colour over the young surgeon's cheekbones. Her only problem was knowing how to answer his question without going into personal matters she had no wish to discuss.

'No, Forrester is not a very common name and I am not married. . .' She paused, wondering whether she should say anything further, but apparently Dr Lu didn't need any further clarification.

'I will see you tonight, then.' He beamed his delight and left with the rest of the group.

'This is no time to be collecting scalps,' Joan teased as she handed Sian a bucket. 'This isn't a hospital with a squad of cleaners coming in after you've finished. On Orbis, you mucky lot have to clean up your own messes!'

Sian groaned good-naturedly as she carried her burden towards the operating theatre.

'I can't say I wasn't warned about this,' she agreed. 'In some ways I think it might be a good idea if some of the surgeons back home did a stint like this. It would certainly make them appreciate the less glamorous side of the job—especially if they're the prima donna type who manage to litter the whole room during a "performance"!'

'You're telling me!' one of the other nurses joined in. 'I remember one man I worked with. . .'

The clean-up operation continued, accompanied by the sort of insider gossip which was probably universal throughout medical circles.

Walls and floors were cleaned down, sinks scrubbed and instruments were loaded into the gas steriliser.

'This steriliser has been a great improvement,' Liz commented, as she and Ann were checking each item on a list. 'On the DC-8, all the metal items were steam-sterilised in "little sisters". Anything with a plastic handle was washed and packaged into plastic bags with an ampoule of ethylene oxide gas. As we left the plane each night, the last person out would break the glass ampoules.'

'What about the next day? Wasn't there a residue of gas in the plane?'

'The first thing we did was let down the generator and start it up. After ten minutes any gas would have been expelled from the plane.'

As they were talking, cartons and packages of supplies were being retrieved from the storage areas in the plane's belly and carried up into the plane itself to replenish stocks ready for the morning.

'Sian.' Joan collared her just as she finished her task. 'Can you stick your head out and let someone know we'll need some more four-oh silk and some twenty and twenty-five needles?'

'No problem,' Sian agreed, and stripped off her booties and cap as she made her way towards the back to change out of her scrubs.

As she stepped out on to the top of the steps, the late afternoon breeze ruffled her hair. The cool air was more then welcome on the damp strands which had been flattened by a disposable hat for most of the day.

Under the plane, the four LD3 containers partially blocked her view of the two gaping entrances into the storage space.

An aluminium ladder was clipped to the rail at the

edge of one opening and, as she moved towards it, a head appeared and identified itself as the nurse-anaesthetist.

· 'Hi!' he mouthed over the noise of the generator, and beckoned her up the ladder.

Sian climbed until her head and shoulders were swallowed into the comparative gloom.

'Wow!' She gazed round at the neatly stacked supplies, amazed that all this had been hidden under her feet all day. 'Is all this needed on one mission?'

'I'm afraid that's wishful thinking.' He shook his head. 'There's a second section——' he pointed with his thumb in the direction of the other opening in the belly of the plane '—and that contains even more in it than this one. We need two deliveries of supplies per mission—things like sterile water, disposables, et cetera. . .' He shrugged.

'It's mind-boggling when you bring it down to packets of needles and four-oh silk, isn't it?' Sian marvelled. 'The sheer scale of the organisation required to keep everything running smoothly. . .'

'What did they send you into the bowels for?' His teeth gleamed whitely in the reflected sunlight.

Sian delivered her message and returned with the requisite packages, unable to help voicing her amazement at the volume of supplies needed to keep Orbis functioning.

'That doesn't take into consideration the work which goes on in the hospitals while we're here,' Joan elaborated. 'Sometimes classes are organised with the surgeons practising the new techniques on sheep or pig's eyes. In some countries the surgeons have never even watched an operation being done under a microscope, let alone training for it themselves.'

Finally, the plane was re-stocked and cleaned ready for the morning and they all climbed into the bus for the return journey to the hotel.

'I hope they're ready for every room to demand a bath full of hot water as soon as we arrive,' Liz quipped. 'It'll take at least an hour's soak before I feel human enough to socialise tonight.'

'Hey!' Ann, her temporary room-mate, dug her in the ribs. 'If you're stuck in there for an hour, when am I going to get my turn?'

'I'll toss you for it.' Liz fished in the pocket of her jeans and drew out a small coin. 'Heads I go first, tails you go first. . .'

'Not until I see that coin.' Ann made a grab for it but narrowly missed. 'I've heard about your lucky coin and I reckon it's got two heads on it.'

The amicable bickering continued throughout the journey, the situation finally being decided on a turn-and-turn-about basis on alternate nights when each rejected the suggestion of sharing simultaneously.

Sian's imagination was fired by the idea and her eyes were drawn towards Sam, her own personal radar somehow knowing exactly where he was without needing to search for his distinctive dark hair and broad shoulders.

Instantly her mind was filled with visions of Sam's body, naked and darkly gleaming as he lazed indolently in the opulence of a large bath full of steaming water. It was all too easy to add her own body to the scene, smaller and paler, her legs entangled with his, her arms twining around his neck to furrow slender fingers through the damp strands which always fell forward over his forehead.

The only problem was that she couldn't tell whether

the images in her mind were wishful fantasies or the replaying of all too accurate memories of happier days.

She gave herself a mental shake as they drew up in front of the hotel. It was going to be hard enough coping with Sam for the rest of the week in such close confines without having to deal with lurid mental images at the same time.

As it happened, Sam was apparently delayed talking to one of the biomedical engineers, and Sian took advantage of the fact to dive straight into the bathroom. By the time Sam arrived, she had returned to the bedroom wearing a hastily donned robe over her rather revealing underwear, while she rubbed her wet hair with a towel.

'Bathroom's all yours,' she said, smiling brightly at his reflection in the mirror to hide her reaction to his presence.

His verbal attack on her after the operation this morning had hurt her deeply. She had believed that she had come to terms with his opinion of her—had wept bitterly that he should have known so little about her that he could think her capable of such utter selfishness that she could have. . .

'Sian?'

Sam's voice broke into her musings and her eyes jerked up to meet his in the mirror as he stood in the doorway of the bathroom.

'What?' Her voice was little-girl breathless as she took in his appearance. How long had she been sitting there lost in thought?

His legs were hidden inside the sharply creased charcoal-grey trousers, the muscles of his thighs only revealed by his smooth-striding approach.

'Can you sort this out for me?'

As he walked towards her, she turned around on the stool, her robe parting company to slide open over one slender thigh, but she scarcely noticed, her attention drawn by the darkly furred chest exposed between the open sides of his pristine white shirt.

His hands appeared in front of her face.

'There seems to be a cotton caught around the cuff-link so that it won't fasten properly.' He relinquished the problem to her, leaving her wondering if she would be any better at solving it, with her hands trembling the way they were.

She took hold of his cuff, making certain that she didn't touch his hand for fear he would sense her turmoil.

The scent of his skin rose up to meet her, an amalgam of the soap he used and the musky smell that was his alone—a combination she would recognise forever.

'You still. . .'

'You smell the same. . .'

They started to speak together and ended up laughing, even though the humour had a touch of melancholy.

'We're still doing it.' Sian's voice was husky with the memories of how many times they had done the same thing. She had always believed that it was a good omen. That it meant they thought alike and would therefore have a much stronger marriage, a much greater chance of making it work.

'You still wear the same perfume, still use the same soap and shampoo.' His free hand came up to her head to touch the tousled strands.

'So do you. . .' she whispered, mesmerised by the gossamer gentleness of his fingertips as he ran them through the dark, damp profusion.

A sharp electronic bleep startled them both, and Sam withdrew his hand to reach across to pick up his watch and wrap it around his hair-sprinkled wrist.

'We've got half an hour before the transport leaves for the reception.' He stepped back and inspected his cuff. 'Thanks for sorting this out.' He indicated the cuff-link, then concentrated on fastening the buttons on his shirt and tucking the tails rapidly into his trousers.

Sian had always joked with him that men could dress faster than women, but this time it was as if he was trying for a world record—as if he couldn't bear to be in the same room as she was for another minute.

As she watched in amazement, he expertly tied a Windsor knot in what looked like a pure silk tie, and shrugged his arms into his jacket while he slid his feet into gleaming black shoes. The brisk wielding of a hairbrush tamed his unruly damp hair, and a fresh handkerchief was tucked into his pocket before he picked up his wallet and key.

'I'll see you downstairs,' he said gruffly, throwing the words to the room at large as he strode towards the door.

The room echoed emptily with the sharp click of the latch as he pulled it closed behind him.

'Oh, Sam,' she whispered. 'How did we end up like this? It was all so perfect once. . .'

She closed her eyes tightly against the tears which burned behind them, and swallowed hard, concentrating on keeping her breathing even while she waited for her pulse-rate to settle.

'That's enough!' she said aloud, her voice banishing the lonely echoes. 'It was his fault just as much as mine. It takes two peole to make a marriage; two people who love each other and trust each other. When the trust dies. . .' She drew in a deep breath and opened her eyes wide in an attempt to dispel the threatening tears before she started to put on her make-up.

The outfit she chose to wear was a matching camisole and sarong skirt in a softly draping silk which, together, looked like a cocktail dress. The emerald and sapphire swirls on a background of black set off the honey tones of her skin to perfection, and her matching slender black heels made her legs seem endless.

It was not until she saw Sam's face as she walked towards him that she remembered he had chosen the outfit for her.

'You'll look like a princess in it, but I'll know how easy it is to take it off you,' he had growled in her ear when she had modelled it for him.

Suddenly she felt a searing heat rising over her cheekbones as she also remembered that she had wickedly intended wearing it with the bare minimum of underwear when she wore it for the first time, and had planned to taunt him with the fact all evening. . .

She had never had the chance to put her plan into action. Just one week later they had parted company and each of them had taken great pains to avoid meeting ever since.

The reception was a very elegant affair attended by several officials from the Ministry of Health as well as representatives of the ophthalmic departments of the local hospitals and the two eye banks in Beijing.

As many of these were accompanied by their part-ners, there was quite a gauntlet for the Orbis team to run.

Here and there Sian thought she recognised a familiar face from the team who had assisted in the operating-room on Orbis, but she had become separated from the rest of the OR team and didn't want to risk embarrassing a complete stranger.

'Doctor.' The soft voice came from behind her and she turned to discover Dr Lu.

'Hello.' She smiled wholeheartedly at him. 'I'm glad to see someone whose English is better than my Chinese; in fact, everyone in this room probably speaks better English than I do!'

'Ah, but you are a better eye-surgeon than they are, so there is a harmonious balance.' He smiled and gestured towards the eminent assembly. 'Would you like me to introduce you to anyone in particular?'

Sian allowed her eyes to wander across the room, and was just about to voice a polite refusal when her gaze was caught by the two men speaking together just inside the ornate doors.

The two of them were easily the tallest in the room, their heights almost equal, as were the serious expressions on their faces.

'Do you know who that is talking to Sam—to Dr Forrester?'

There was silence for a moment, and when she glanced towards Dr Lu it was to see a bemused frown on his face.

'But that is your own Mr Oliver Foot. He is the president and executive director of Orbis.'

'Ah.' She nodded. 'I know about him, of course, but I haven't met him yet.'

Sian's eyes were drawn back to the pair of them, struck again by the similarities between them. They both carried themselves with a quiet air of command as if they possessed an innate knowledge of their own worth and the value of their chosen work.

As she watched them talking together Sian realised that, even though she was unable to hear what they were discussing, she could tell that they had found kindred spirits in each other.

Suddenly they laughed, deep-chested masculine laughter, their faces alight with a similar almost boyish glee, and Sian realised that it was the first time since they had arrived in China that she had seen Sam without an air of strain.

This was the man she had fallen in love with, the man she had married. An intense man, dedicated to his career, but also a considerate man with a love of the traditional values of home and family, combined with a wicked sense of humour and more unconscious sex appeal than one man deserved.

They had been so well-matched, for she had dedicated herself to the same goals, the same ideals as he had. . .

'Would you like me to introduce you to Mr Foot?'

The quiet question startled her. She had all but forgotten that Dr Lu was standing beside her.

'I do apologise,' she murmured, feeling the heat rise in her cheeks. 'Please forgive my rudeness but I was thinking. . .' Her voice tailed off helplessly.

'You were thinking how much alike the two of them are?' he questioned softly, and smiled when he saw her jerk of amazement. 'The likeness is so strong that I would not be surprised if they were of the same horoscope sign.'

They also shared the same dark, intent gaze under dark, strongly marked eyebrows which Sian suddenly found focused in her direction.

The sensation was rather like finding herself the subject under one of Orbis' operating microscopes.

As she watched, Oliver turned briefly towards Sam and smiled while he spoke a few words, then held his hand out in a friendly gesture of farewell before his attention was claimed by a small group of eminent-looking Chinese men and their quietly elegant wives.

Sam's attention returned to Sian and her companion, and he made his way towards them through the throng.

'Dr Lu.' Sam nodded formally and held out his hand. 'Will you be operating again tomorrow?'

'No, not tomorrow. I was fortunate today that my patient was chosen as a good demonstration case. I have learnt a great deal working with Dr Forrester these last two days.' He turned towards Sian and bowed slightly.

'The operation went very smoothly——' Sam smiled '—in spite of the less than ordinary circumstances.'

Before Dr Lu could continue the conversation, a young woman in a dark skirt and white blouse came to stand beside him. The small badge on her lapel identified her as an interpreter.

'Excuse me, please. May I ask if Dr Lu could come to speak with a gentleman from the ministry? He is talking to Mr Foot about the operations today.'

Dr Lu turned to Sian and smiled. 'It should be you who speaks, not I——'

'Not at all,' Sam interrupted. 'Mr Foot will probably be speaking to Dr Forrester later this evening or tomorrow. I think that this time it is your opinions which will be valuable.'

Dr Lu acquiesced with a smile and wished them a good evening.

'I think he's quite taken with you,' Sam murmured, so softly that only Sian could hear.

'Wh-what?' she breathed in astonishment.

'I don't blame him, seeing you in that outfit.' He

turned his head towards her briefly and allowed his eyes to drift over her. To anyone watching him it would seem totally casual, but Sian felt as if she had been scorched from head to foot.

'I remember the day we bought it.' His voice had taken on a gravelly roughness. 'All I could think about was that it would look stunning if you wore it with the minimum underneath, but if you ever dared to do it I would probably go insane before the evening was over.'

Sian drew in a sharp breath as the shock hit her, and a trembling feeling started deep inside her as she raised her eyes slowly to meet his.

'My God,' he muttered, when he saw her expression and read the confirmation in it. 'You actually thought of doing it?' A dark tide of colour swept along the planes of his cheekbones as his eyes flicked rapidly downwards, then back up to her face again. 'You didn't. . .?'

She shook her head once, a feeling uncurling inside her which was equal parts shock and excitement. It was a feeling which only Sam had ever incited.

'Sian. . .' With visible reluctance he dragged his eyes away from hers and shot his cuff back to look at his watch.

'How much longer is this supposed to go on?' he muttered fiercely, as he shoved his fisted hands into his trouser pockets and turned until he was partially hidden from the room by her body.

Sian followed the movement and suddenly realised that it had a serious purpose. Her heart gave a wildly uneven thump as she realised that Sam had been aroused by their conversation.

'Stop looking at me like that or I'll disgrace us all,' he hissed through gritted teeth.

She smiled slyly up at him as a trickle of awareness became a flash flood.

'Would you rather I went to talk to someone else?'

'Don't you dare.' There was a slight sheen across his forehead and a touch of panic in his voice. 'You stand right where you are until I'm fit for polite company.'

'How long will that take?' she asked innocently as she brushed her arm surreptitiously against his.

'Forever, if you keep that up. . .' His voice had become decidedly husky. Just the sound of it was enough to make her heart beat faster, her skin tingling as if he was stroking it with velvet.

'Sam. . .' she whispered as her eyes sought his, knowing they would tell him of her confusion.

'We need to talk.' He ran the tips of his fingers over the back of her hand. 'When we get back to the hotel. There must be some way we can——'

'Ladies and gentlemen. . .' The announcement cut across his words, inviting them through to an adjoining room where an entertainment would be presented for them.

Sam quickly placed his hand on the back of her waist, ostensibly to usher her across the room, and he chose their seats carefully.

Only Sian knew that his fingers were surreptitiously caressing her as he settled her in her seat, sliding across the silky fabric until he determined that she wasn't wearing a bra, then silently taunting her with the knowledge with an 'accidental' contact with the aroused evidence of her breast.

The next hour was a refined blend of delight and torture for Sian. The entertainment was a wonderful example of traditional Chinese music and dance, but her concentration was spoilt by Sam's close proximity. His nearness was exciting, keeping her nerves at fever pitch, but apprehension grew as she realised that she was no closer to knowing his true feelings about her.

He had said that they needed to talk and it was obvious that he intended to have that discussion tonight. The only problem was the fierce attraction which seemed to have re-kindled between them.

She had no way of knowing whether they were both under the influence of raging hormones, aided and abetted by proximity, or whether this was the explosive start of a whole new beginning.

At last the Orbis crew were able to take their leave of their hosts, Sian and Sam guiltily aware that neither of them had been able to appreciate the entertainment properly with their minds almost fully occupied with their own thoughts.

The bus was waiting outside, manned by their usual driver, Mr Cheung, who was still smiling as widely as ever in spite of his long day.

Sam did some clever manoeuvering and managed to secure the pair of seats closest to the door.

'Ready for a quick getaway,' he muttered with a wicked grin.

Sian tried to concentrate on the passing scenery, hearing someone say that they were somewhere near the Lake of Ten Monasteries. She knew that she was unlikely to visit Beijing again, but all she could think about was the fact that Sam had captured her hand and threaded his fingers through hers. His thumb was stroking gently over her knuckles, sending delicate shivers up her arm until the tiny hairs stood up on the back of her neck.

The crash was fierce and totally unexpected, leaving the bus slewed across a junction. The silence which followed was uncanny after the cacophony of the impact.

'Did you see that?' A voice rose incredulously. 'They shot across without looking and. . . Hey! They're running away!'

To Sian's amazement, she saw the occupants of the car now embedded firmly in the side of the bus scramble out of their ruined vehicle and sprint back along the road. Within seconds they had disappeared from sight.

'Is everyone all right?' Sam stood in the centre aisle and called for attention.

There were some moans and groans, but it seemed as if they had all escaped unscathed until Liz spoke up in a worried voice.

'Steve's bleeding.' She was quickly assessing the damage. 'I think he's just caught the side of his head on the edge of the window but it's bleeding quite a lot.'

At that point the police arrived on the scene and there was a great deal of very heated shouting and arm-waving going on before Mr Cheung had each arm grabbed by a policeman and was frog-marched towards the police car.

'Hey! What's going on?' Sam demanded from his position by the door.

The group paused long enough for one of their number to call something back towards the bus before they continued to march the unfortunate Mr Cheung away.

'Just a minute,' he called again, and leapt agilely down the steps, closely followed by a very agitated translator.

'Please. Sir.' She was clasping her hands tightly together and looking hopefully over her shoulder towards the bus, as if longing for the mission manager to hurry over to help her. 'It is best you do not make yourself responsible for this man.'

Sam stopped so suddenly that she nearly crashed into his broad back.

'Will you translate for me?' he demanded.

'Of course, sir.' She nodded frantically. 'But——'

'Sam,' the mission manager began, her voice pitched at a persuasive level. Sam held one imperative hand up towards her and Celia paused while he asked his question.

'Ask the policemen why they are taking Mr Cheung away.'

There was a rapid exchange of words before the translator reported back.

'There has been an accident and they must arrest the driver.'

'But he did not cause the accident,' Sam objected. 'The other men ran away.'

'I know,' she said weakly. 'So they must arrest someone until they can find——'

'That's ludicrous,' he snapped rudely. 'Tell them that Mr Cheung has done nothing wrong. That I vouch for his innocence personally. Tell them that he is the official bus driver for the visiting surgeons and staff of Orbis International.' He folded his arms ominously across his chest, a stern expression pulling his dark brows down over his eyes.

Sian had followed him out of the bus and was standing quietly to one side, watching the flood of words which flowed between the police, the translator and the unfortunate Mr Cheung.

Finally, grudgingly, the police relinquished the poor man, apparently impressed with the importance of avoiding an incident with such important visitors, and set about making arrangements to clear the obstruction.

'There will be a bus coming to take everyone to the hotel,' the translator announced. 'If you would all like to wait inside the bus until it comes.' She glanced around at the semi-circle of people. Most of the team had left the bus in the hope of seeing justice done, and were delighted with the outcome. Mr Cheung had impressed them all by his friendly nature, and several of the crew patted him on he shoulder in congratulation.

As they all straggled back inside, they were greeted by Liz.

'What are we going to do about Steve's head? It's still losing quite a lot and the cut really needs stiching.'

The medical director conferred with Celia and the poor Chinese translator before raising his voice in a request.

'Any volunteers to take Steve back to Orbis to sew him back together? We'll lay on a taxi each way, but it will mean that you'll be that much later getting to the hotel.'

'I'm not on till tomorrow afternoon,' Sam said helpfully.

'And I'm the floating member of staff tomorrow,' added Liz.

'Thank you.' He smiled. 'It shouldn't take long to open Orbis up long enough to put him back together and then lock everything up again. It'll be much faster than taking him to a local hospital and we'll be using our own resources.'

The decisions made, everyone sat back down to wait.

'Sam,' Sian said quietly. 'I might as well come with you rather than go back to the hotel alone. . .'

He smiled ruefully as he reached for her hand.

'Not exactly the ending we had in mind for tonight, is it?' he murmured so that only she could hear. 'Well, maybe it's all for the best. At least this way we're more likely to sit down and talk before we get totally carried away and maybe make a worse mistake than we did the last time.'

Sian's heart sank into her elegantly shod feet. After all her high hopes, it sounded as if Sam was regretting the things he had said, the things he had hinted as he slowly drove her mad all evening with no more than his voice and the touch of his hand.

'Would you rather I went back to the hotel?' She kept her voice expressionless but it was an effort.

'There's no point in both of us missing our sleep, especially as you're one of the first in the firing line tomorrow morning,' he said, sounding so coolly logical and reasonable that Sian wanted to shake him. 'You might as well take advantage of the bathroom while you can.' And he leant back calmly in his seat to wait for the taxi to arrive.

'He said we needed to talk,' she muttered, as she dumped her key on the dressing-table and kicked her shoes off. 'Then, just when I'm beginning to hope that we'll be able to get everything sorted out, he gets cold feet.'

She stripped off her lovely silky outfit, pulling a face at it as she hung it away carefully.

She had wondered if he would remember that he had chosen it for her; wondered if it would still have the same effect on her as it had two years ago. If anything, the power of his reaction was stronger than ever, if his degree of arousal was anything to go by.

If only the accident hadn't happened. They could have been. . . What? Suddenly she put the brakes on her imagination.

What was she thinking of? She and Sam were no longer married and, in spite of the fact that the attraction between them seemed to be more potent than ever, they still had a huge chasm of misunderstanding dividing them.

Her disappointment left her feeling hollow inside but, as she climbed into bed in the silent loneliness of the room, she had to admit that Sam had been right about one thing—they needed to talk.

CHAPTER FIVE

SIAN was just tucking her hair inside her disposable cap the next day when there was a minor disturbance at the top of the steps.

Hearing childish voices raised in anger, she made her way to the door to see what was happening, just as a group of children scrambled down the steps, leaving one of their number behind.

'Hey!' she said softly, as she bent down to the child huddled into a sobbing heap. 'What's the matter?' She ran her hand over the tangled darkness of thick straight hair and tilted a little pointed chin upwards to see tear-tracks over dark gold, grimy cheeks. He refused to look up at her, shaking his head and keeping his eyes firmly hidden behind short straight black lashes.

'Ann?' she called over her shoulder to the nurse on duty in the nearby recovery-room. 'Is there a translator on board yet? If so, could you ask if they could come back here for a second?'

A few minutes later there was the sound of footsteps coming along the corridor from the class-room at the front of the plane towards the rear entrance where Sian was still kneeling.

'Please, how can I help you?'

It was the soft voice of the same young woman who had been on the bus the night before, and she gave Sian a friendly smile of recognition.

'Could you ask him why he's crying, please?' Sian requested, her heart going out to the little waif.

After a hesitant start, the young lad started speaking as he was gently coaxed.

'Apparently the argument started because his friends wanted to see what was going on in the plane,' the translator explained. 'They said that Chou was in the way and there was no point in him spoiling their view because he couldn't see properly anyway.'

'Can you ask him to look at me,' Sian asked, as she gently urged him again to raise his chin.

Long practice meant that she didn't allow her feelings to show on her face, but in this instance it was a struggle to appear impassive when she saw the condition of his eyes.

'Did he come to the hospital for screening the other day?' She tilted his head from side to side and estimated the reaction of his pupils to light by shading them alternately with her hand.

She couldn't remember seeing him before, but there had been so many people. . .

'He says he wanted to come but his grandfather was ill so he had to stay home with his little brother.'

'Couldn't one of his parents have brought him?'

Once again her questions were laboriously translated and the answer relayed.

'He says his parents are dead. There is only his grandfather and his brother.'

'Does he have to look after his little brother while his grandfather goes to work? How does he manage with his eyes so bad?'

While continuing with the preparations for the morning surgery, Liz had seen what was happening by the door and brought Sian's bag out to her, a sympathetic grimace on her face.

'He says,' the translator replied, 'that his grandfather

is old and cannot see at all. Chou, here, has to go to work so that they can eat.'

'How old is he?' Sian's heart felt heavy.

'He is eleven.'

'Is there no one he can go to for help?' She chose her words carefully, not wanting the young woman to think she was being critical.

There was an extended bout of rapid-fire questions, with Chou alternately frightened and defiant.

'He says that when his grandfather went blind, he didn't dare notify anyone because he was afraid that his grandsons would be taken away. Then, when Chou's eyes start to fail, he made his brother promise not to tell Grandfather.'

Such a simple tale of misconceptions and yet it had caused so much misery.

Sian looked up from her examination to catch Liz's eye.

'Could you ask the medical director if I can see him for a moment?' Sian smiled bleakly up at the translator, her soft blue eyes filled with sadness. 'He is blind in one eye,' she explained briefly as she stroked his hair softly, 'and he is losing the sight in the other one.'

The strange little group waited patiently at the top of the steps, their clothes fluttering in the fitful breeze of a beautiful day, the sky cloudless and bleached pale blue by the brightness of the sun.

Sian gazed around, conscious that the child in front of her couldn't see any of that beauty; his sight had already deteriorated so far.

When the medical director arrived, Sian explained what she had learned about Chou.

'He was unable to attend the screening session at the hospital but, please, may I take him through to the examination-room to see if he's a suitable case for surgery?'

He was already shaking his head as he glanced down at his watch.

'It can't be done.' His tone was regretful. 'Not today, with the particular cases we already have prepped and waiting.'

'What about lunchtime?' she pleaded. 'If he comes back later on, could we check him through?'

There was a long silence.

'Orbis can't take on every case, Sian. That's not the reason why we travel around the world like this.'

'I know,' she agreed, clasping her hands tightly together as she fought to rally her argument. 'But Chou didn't even get a chance to be seen because he was taking care of his family at eleven years of age. At least let me take a look at him. . .please?'

This time the silence stretched on even longer before a wry smile crossed his face.

'Usually it's the host doctors who beg for just one more patient to be seen, just one more fitted into the operating schedule. I don't usually have to put up with mutiny in the camp from our own staff!'

'So I can see him midday?' Her voice lifted with hope. 'He can come back later this morning?'

'Yes,' he agreed fatalistically. 'He can come in first thing this afternoon so you can run the tests before the first scheduled case starts.'

'Thank you!' Sian captured one of his hands and clasped it tight between both of hers as her heart lifted with hope. 'Thank you so much.'

'You know, of course, that there is no guarantee that his condition is operable, nor that we would be able to do anything about it if it was,' he warned as he straightened up.

'Yes. I understand,' she agreed. 'But at least he will have been seen, and any diagnosis can be passed on to the host doctors so that he can be treated that much earlier.'

The medical director's hand patted her on the shoulder as he smiled sympathetically before turning to make his way back along the corridor towards the class-room.

She turned to the translator, who had been quietly talking to the young lad throughout the exchange. 'Please could you explain to Chou that he must come back to the plane after lunch? Then we can do all the tests to find out if anything can be done for his eyes.'

Sian waited while her words were relayed to the young lad. He was still sitting in the corner of the platform at the top of the steps, the tracks of his tears now dry on his dusty cheeks.

His face was still almost totally impassive as he nodded several times, and Sian suddenly found herself wondering what he would look like if he were to smile the way an eleven-year-old should smile. But then, she reminded herself, he hadn't a great deal to smile about at the moment.

Surreptitiously, she crossed her fingers for luck as she watched him hold tightly to the rail as he made his way down the steps, hoping that this afternoon would be the start of a brighter future for him.

Back inside Orbis, she made her way forward to the monitor. Philip had just started an illustrated presentation of laser techniques until the next patient was ready in the operating theatre.

'We realise that there are very few ophthalmic lasers

in the hospitals in China yet,' he was saying. 'This is the same for most hospitals in the world, especially as laser technology is such a new branch of ophthalmic surgery. . .' Philip had addressed his audience in general terms, and Sian watched the host doctors nodding vigorously when his comments were translated.

'This is part of the purpose of Orbis,' he continued. 'When we are invited to visit, there is a great deal of media interest because of the novelty of the idea. This means that many people will hear of the things which are possible in modern ophthalmology, such as government ministers and hospital administrators. . .' He paused as a ripple of laughter ran around the classroom.

'Then, when you ask for the funds to buy an ophthalmic laser for your hospital, there is a much better chance that they will know what it is and why you need it.'

Having finished his introduction, he signalled for the audio-visual department to start running the tape.

'The next important purpose of Orbis is to share knowledge. . .' There was another round of approving nods. 'It is impossible for everyone to travel around the world to train with the best equipment and learn the latest techniques under the world's best surgeons, so Orbis brings it to the world.'

The tape which followed had the audience enthralled as it showed the laser treatment of cloudy corneas after cataract removal, followed by a section on the treatment of open-angle glaucoma by using the laser to 'unplug' the drainage system of the eye and so prevent blindness.

The second half of the tape demonstrated the use of lasers to correct the damage caused to the eye by diabetes and detailed the system for 'stitching' a

detached retina back in position with anything from
three hundred to four hundred separate tiny burns.

The discussion at the end of the presentation was
fierce, with the host doctors asking extremely detailed
questions about the diagnosis and prognosis of suitable
cases and the present success rate, and was only called
to a halt when the signal came that the next case was
ready for live transmission from the operating theatre.

Sian had been just as impressed with the presentation
as her Chinese colleagues. As a specialist in paediatric
ophthalmic surgery, she knew the particular range of
conditions which she could see time after time in her
young patients.

Her time on Orbis was giving her the chance not only
to pass on her own expertise but also to brush up on
other techniques which she would not often need to use.

Although it was sad to see so much evidence of
serious eye disease, the whole experience was
exhilarating.

Unfortunately for her peace of mind, she was also
being thrown into contact with Sam nearly twenty-four
hours a day.

This morning, she had woken early to find him still
deeply asleep, and had been unable to resist the opportunity to gaze her fill.

The sheet had slipped down to his waist, revealing a
broad expanse of tanned shoulder and muscular arm,
his hand loosely clenched on the pillow beside his face.
In sleep he still looked the same as when she had first
met him, all tension smoothed away to give him a
touching air of innocence.

His dark hair had been rumpled, one thick strand
lying across his forehead to touch his eyebrow, and her
fingers had itched to smooth it back; to run through the

silky mass and trace the shape of his head; to cradle him against her the way she had when they had. . .

She had turned away and slipped silently out of her bed and into the bathroom, grabbing a pair of light cotton trousers and a matching apricot polo-shirt on the way past.

Much as she dreaded the pain of opening up the old wounds which talking would cause, if she had reached across to touch him he would have woken, and the last thing on their minds would have been talking.

He had still been sleeping by the time she had dressed, and she had left the room before she could give in to the temptation to join him in his bed, to slide under the covers with him and explore the naked body which was hidden there.

She had been grateful to find herself the first member of the team to come down that morning, so that she would not be forced to make conversation.

While she had her very early breakfast she had fought a battle with herself over her relationship with Sam.

I know he still wants me and, God knows, I still want him, but is that enough? she had agonised under her breath. How can I ask him if he still loves me? And if he doesn't, is there any chance that he could grow to love me again?

The questions had run round and round in her head like mice condemned to a treadmill.

In the end, the only thing she could be sure of was her own feelings. She had loved Sam Forrester from the day she had met him and, in spite of the fact that he had broken her heart with his cruel accusations and his lack of trust, she had never stopped loving him.

All she could do now was wait and hope.

There was no official event planned for the evening

and an outing had been planned for the whole team to do some sightseeing in Beijing at the end of the afternoon session.

Briefly, she allowed her thoughts to run ahead of her to the evening still to come.

Perhaps she would have the chance to spend some time with Sam. Perhaps, if they took the opportunity during the next few days to get to know each other again, it could be like the happy times when they had just met and anything was possible.

When lunchtime arrived, Sian sat in the shade under Orbis with one eye directed towards the airport buildings. Although he was just one child among the many she had seen, there was something about Chou which had tugged at her heartstrings, and she couldn't help the excitement building at the possibility of helping him.

The headphones she wore against the constant noise of the generator gave her the excuse to sit quietly thinking her own thoughts as she waited to see him make his way across the open expanse at the side of runway.

Gradually she became concerned as she checked her watch and saw the time trickling away, and tried to find the translator who had spoken to Chou.

'Soon Yi will be here tomorrow,' her fellow-translator confirmed, with a smile which did nothing to alleviate Sian's frustration.

The afternoon session began, leaving Sian with a crushing sense of disappointment.

Where was Chou? Had something happened to him, or was there a problem with his family?

For the rest of the afternoon she was on tenterhooks,

glancing out of the windows at odd moments in the hope of seeing Chou on his way to the plane.

Gradually, as the busy afternoon flew past, her optimism faded until, in the end, she had to admit that he wasn't going to arrive.

Several times she had noticed Sam looking at her, his gaze quizzical, but she didn't want to talk to him until she knew for certain. . .

She pulled herself up short, amazed at the turn of her thoughts.

In spite of the fact that she and Sam were divorced, she knew that he would understand her feelings when she told him of her disappointment over Chou.

He had always understood — her hopes, her ambitions, her fears. *That* was one of the things which had hurt her so badly two years ago — that he could have known her so well, and yet not have known her at all. . . not have trusted her.

The clean-up at the end of surgery went even faster than the previous day, the team starting to work well together as a unit in spite of the occasional moan.

'You'd better be careful, Sian,' Ann warned as they travelled back to the hotel. 'Each new group of surgeons does their best to wriggle out of mopping up in OR. With a female among them, they'll do their best to leave it up to you!'

'I'm sure I'll manage to find some way of evening things up.' Sian smiled, her attitude deliberately upbeat.

All day, in spite of her preoccupation with Chou and her disappointment that he hadn't returned, she had been vibrantly aware that Sam was only a few feet away from her.

During her time in the operating-room she had known that he was watching her on the monitors, and she found herself lifted by the knowledge, her words and technique flowing effortlessly.

When it was his turn in the theatre, she had been riveted to the screen, silently applauding his skill and clarity at the end of yet another successful operation. She had always admired his dedication, understanding his intensity easily because she was equally ambitious.

Unfortunately, the ambition which had drawn them so closely together had also been the instrument which had driven them apart.

For two years Sian had believed that she hated Sam, her heart filled with the pain of broken trust. It had only taken three days in his company for her to realise that her love had only been hidden under the hurt, waiting for the chance to flourish again.

Now she needed to talk to Sam; to find out what his feelings were.

She had missed him so much the last two years. Missed his wry sense of humour, his intensity about his work, the almost miraculous way he would seem to know what she was thinking, what she was feeling. . .

Sian raced through her preparations for the sightseeing trip, expecting Sam to arrive at any moment.

She brushed her hair vigorously, noted that it was nearly time for another trim, then paused, wondering with a pang of regret whether to grow it again. Sam had loved her long hair. . .

She stepped back from the mirror and cast a quick glance over herself. The aqua-and-white trouser-suit was cool and light in a fine pure cotton, the low-heeled sandals would be comfortable for walking, and the cotton knit cardigan would be enough to throw round her shoulders if the temperature dropped later.

Finally, she couldn't wait for him any longer without missing the trip, no matter how badly she wanted a few minutes alone with him before she had to share him with the rest of the team.

She picked up her key and, confirming that her small emergency purse was tucked in her pocket, she left the room and made her way down to the reception area.

The first person she saw as the lift doors opened was Sam, her eyes drawn instantly to his lean dark height by the force of his presence. It was as if he was the only person in the room.

He was wearing the same short-sleeved blue shirt and stone-coloured trousers as that morning, but his dark hair was still damp and his jaw was newly shaven.

Sian felt a sharp pang. Where had he gone to freshen up? Why had he not come back to their room? Didn't he know that she wanted to talk to him—*needed* to talk to him?

She made her way across the elegantly appointed room, a tremulous smile hovering on her lips as she waited for him to notice her.

As she joined the group, he glanced in her direction and then looked away again as if she was a stranger.

Sian felt the blood drain out of her cheeks, as shocked as if he had slapped her in the face. She took a stumbling step backwards and whirled away. All she could think about was escaping back to their room.

So much for her hopes that they were on the verge of finding each other after two years of misery.

Her eyes were stinging and she blinked furiously, calling on her professional poise in her determination not to let him see her cry.

'Ladies and gentlemen.' Celia's clear voice called for their attention. 'The bus is waiting outside the front of the hotel.'

The resulting surge of bodies carried Sian away from the lifts and out of the imposing front entrance of the hotel.

'Come on, Sian.' Joan's voice reached her as Sian hesitated briefly at the steps of the bus. 'Let's see if they've left the back seats free. I always wanted to be one of the gang sitting at the back when I was at school. They always seemed to have the most fun.'

Her cheerful nonsense carried Sian into the bus and along the gangway right to the back, closely followed by Ann and Liz.

As she passed Sam, their eyes met fleetingly.

If she hadn't once known him as well as she knew herself, she would have thought his expression totally impassive, but she saw the brief flash of heat in his gaze.

The only thing she didn't know was what he was feeling. Was it anger he had quickly hidden? It could hardly be desire after such a pointed snub.

She settled herself in her seat as the doors were closed, determined to ignore the dark-haired, broad-shouldered cause of her misery. This evening she was going to enjoy herself — in spite of him.

'Hey, listen to this.' Liz was flicking through a pile of tourist leaflets she had picked up at the hotel reception desk. 'There's a Restaurant of Accumulated Virtue and another one called the Restaurant of Unbounded Virtue and Happiness.'

Ann was perusing another leaflet. 'There are three altars. The Altar of Earth, Sun and Moon.'

'And there's Wall Street,' Joan chipped in, reading over Liz's shoulder.

'I like the sound of the Thieves' Market.' Sian found herself joining in. 'It sounds as if the Chinese traders are a little more honest than most. At least you know what to expect!'

'Do you think we'll have time to see the Great Wall?' Ann was still unfolding leaflets.

'I don't know whether there'll be time this week, but Orbis will be here for three weeks in all, so it might be possible later on.'

'That's all right for the field staff,' Sian grumbled good-naturedly. 'But we visitors are only here for a week and it's Thursday tomorrow.'

That thought was enough to dampen her enthusiasm in spite of her determination to put her disappointment out of her head. She listened to the translator's description of the history and buildings they were passing, but her feelings were subdued.

In three days, she and Sam would say goodbye to each other again, and this time there would be no chance that coincidence would throw them together again.

The tour took them past the walls to the Forbidden City, but Sian found she could raise little enthusiasm. It was not until they stopped at the Gong Wang Palace that her mood lightened slightly.

The open-sided pavilions and arcaded walkways took her through peaceful gardens of lily-ponds and pomegranate trees.

She wandered on through a silent courtyard and came to the living quarters, the delicate architecture having a strangely soothing effect on her tangled feelings.

She turned a corner, her eyes fixed on a series of brightly painted beams and dark latticed screens, and collided with a figure coming in the opposite direction.

Breathless, she found herself gazing up at Sam; at his dark eyes and tanned features, his hair windblown into disarray. The rapid pulse at the base of her throat was mute evidence of the effect his closeness was having on her. She was certain he must be able to hear her heartbeat from where he stood, but was unable to move a muscle.

For long silent seconds he stared down at her, his eyes curiously hooded, his tense face oddly impassive until he blinked.

'Excuse me,' he muttered shortly, his rigid jaw telling Sian that he was gritting his teeth, the aura of strain around him almost visible as he strode away.

Suddenly, the only thing she wanted to do was go back to the hotel and bury her head under her pillow, her feeling of despair overwhelming her like a black cloud.

She gritted her own teeth, determined not to be a wet blanket on the rest of the team until, finally, it was time to return to the hotel.

Sam was chatting quietly to a group of people in the reception area when Sian passed him on her way to the lifts.

Pride made her lift her chin and walk with a jaunty step until she was out of his sight, but once the lift doors closed she collapsed tiredly against the pristine interior, her shoulders slumped with defeat.

'It's Wednesday evening,' she reminded herself, as she stripped in the bathroom and stepped under the shower. 'Just two days more on Orbis, then I'll be flying home on Saturday. . .' She tilted her face up to the drenching spray and allowed it to stream down over her body.

For several minutes she stood there, lathering shampoo into her hair and luxuriating in the silky feel of the water, but it wasn't long before the memories began to creep in.

Memories of the tiny shower in the first home she and Sam had lived in, and how he had managed to join her in the cramped space on more than one occasion. Memories of the laughter and pleasure they had shared.

Suddenly everything rose up to overwhelm her and, as the first sob echoed around the shower-stall, she wrapped her arms around her own ribs for comfort, realising at last that not all the water running down her face was coming from the shower.

As she huddled against the wall, her mind was filled with a myriad scenes, overloaded beyond bearing with a kaleidoscopic mixture of emotions.

Dimly she knew that this was a natural reaction to the tension she had been under, and the series of events became jumbled as she recalled them.

The sudden journey halfway round the world and the heart-rending scenes of desperate parents begging for their child's sight; the disappointment over Chou's inexplicable non-appearance; above all, the shock of meeting Sam without warning and having to be in such close proximity after the heart-break of the events two years ago.

Sunk deep in misery, she was oblivious to everything but the incessant spray of water, the warmth wrapping her in a womb-like environment as she finally let the grief pour out.

There was something inevitable about the pair of hands which pulled her away from the wall. They turned her until she was circled by familiar arms and pulled against Sam's warm muscular body, one broad palm cradling her head against his shoulder as he pulled the door shut behind him.

For the first time in two years they were shut in the warm confines of a shower together. Somewhere deep in her brain a little voice was trying to tell her that she should be objecting. She should be telling him to get out; he no longer had the right to take such liberties. . . but she didn't have the will-power.

She needed him too much.

Needed the strength of his arms to hold her sob-shaken body upright, needed his broad shoulder to rest her aching head on, needed the comfort of wrapping her arms around him and holding him so tightly that she might never let go.

'Sian?'

His voice was a husky whisper, barely audible over the sound of the water.

'Oh, Sam,' she wailed, burying her face against his neck with a renewed bout of weeping, finally giving into the deep, racking, pain-filled sobs.

His arms tightened around her and he rocked her gently under the soothing stream, his voice an indecipherable rumble of comforting sounds as he smoothed her hair away from her face.

It seemed totally natural that he should drop a kiss on her forehead, totally right that it should be followed by a gentle string of kisses down the side of her face, each one interspersed with words murmured in his deep voice.

Slowly the tears subsided until at last she drew in a shuddering breath and lifted her head to look up at him.

His thick dark lashes were stuck together in clumps, the drops of water accentuating their length and giving his dark eyes an extra shine. His hair was flattened against his head, outlining the shape of his skull, the gleam of water over his skin turning him into a bronzed sculpture of some mythical god.

A sudden uneasiness had her scrambling for words. Any words.

'They'll be running. . .'

'They'll be running out of water. . .' She gave him an ironic smile as they once more spoke together.

'Come on, then.' Sam reach round her to turn the water off, his arm tightening around her as she tried to step aside in the limited space.

She tried to arch away from him to minimise the contact between them, but only succeeded in tantalising herself with the soft friction of her breasts against the dark silky pelt across his chest.

He froze, his eyes fixed on her own until she watched them travel downwards. She knew what he was seeing when he drew in a sharp breath, and knew what he was feeling when she recognised the unmistakable reaction of his body against hers.

In a sudden flurry of movement he pushed the door open to reach for a towel.

'Let's get you dried off before you go wrinkly,' he said in a husky voice, as he wrapped the soft fabric around her gently.

He turned to take a second towel from the rail which he twisted rapidly around his waist before he bent to swing her up into his arms.

'Sam!' she squeaked breathlessly. 'Put me down!'

CHAPTER SIX

'ARE you afraid I'll drop you?' he teased, as he swung her effortlessly through the doorway and into their room, her body cradled firmly against him.

She could hear the laughter in his voice as it rumbled through the depths of his chest, and relished her position, her arms around his neck and her head resting in what was once its customary position on his shoulder.

It was all so frighteningly familiar, as if they had never been apart—as if the last two years were nothing more than a terrible dream.

Sam shifted his hold as he sat down on the bed, and Sian found herself cradled on his lap. One broad palm found its way to her hip to pull her close while the other cupped the side of her head, his fingers stroking through the damp tendrils, smoothing them away from her face.

'I do miss your long hair,' he murmured sadly, his voice not much more than a whisper to stir against her ear.

Suddenly her eyes were stinging again and she was fighting tears. His words had reminded her that two years had passed and everything *had* changed.

'Oh, Sam.' She was unable to prevent a forlorn little sob escaping.

'Hush, now. That's enough, or you'll make yourself sick.' He wrapped both arms around her and rocked her backwards and forwards as if she were a little child.

'It's not fair,' she moaned pathetically. 'Life just isn't fair. . .' The words were trite, but they were the only ones she could find to express her feelings.

Amazingly, she felt Sam shudder, and looked up to catch a strange expression on his face, half-sadness, half-humour.

'Ah, Sian.' He leant forward to press another kiss on her forehead. 'No one ever promised that life would be fair.' He chuckled briefly. 'If only it was. . .'

He buried his face in the side of her neck, nuzzling the tender skin behind her ear before he became still.

The quiet of the room was broken only by the muffled sounds of the hotel's other guests. For the first time in two years Sian felt contentment stealing through her. She had Sam's arms wrapped around her and the soft warmth of his breath stirring the strands of rapidly drying hair against her cheek.

Gradually she became aware that his breathing pattern had changed, and she slowly tilted her head back until she could look at him, finding his eyes waiting for her.

Dark eyes, very dark, the pupils dilating further even as she watched.

'Sian?' Sam drew the tips of his fingers across her cheek until he came to the corner of her mouth. One finger stroked gently over the soft fullness of her lower lip as though exploring the texture of her skin.

Sian felt her heart start to race and her lips seemed to be swelling. Without conscious thought, she flicked out her tongue to moisten them and found his finger.

She paused, the tip of her tongue withdrawing briefly before a sudden surge of courage had her parting her lips again to capture his fingertip and draw it into the darkness.

'God!' he groaned, as she stroked him with her tongue.

He bent his head slowly towards her, watching her,

watching the expression in her eyes, seeing the excitement building.

His gaze flicked down to her mouth as he slowly withdrew his finger far enough to leave a trail of glistening moisture on her lower lip. Then, at the last possible moment, his eyes closed as he swooped to replace his finger with his own tongue.

His kiss was gentle, tantalising, possessive, as if kissing her was all he wanted to do for the rest of his life. Gradually it grew in intensity, deeper, harder, until Sian was breathless, her arms wound tightly around his shoulders, her fingers tangled in the damp thickness of his hair as she held him close.

'Sian?' The hoarse word was a demand and a plea as he drew back far enough for her to see his stormy gaze.

'Oh, Sam,' she breathed, and their mouths came together as explosively as a flash of lightning setting off a forest fire, raw, fiery and endless.

She could hear her own whimpers mingling with Sam's hungry groans as she clung to him in a world gone mad. She'd forgotten how it felt to kiss like this, hot and shivery all at once, and totally out of control.

Sam's hands were stroking her, her shoulders and arms, the slope of her back and the curve of her hip, bringing every one of her nerves back to life.

Her own hands were exploring his body, kneading the muscles of his shoulders and arms, tracing the contours of his back and thrilling at the taut, muscular virility.

She was only vaguely aware of him lifting her until her head met the smooth coolness of the pillow and his body followed her down.

'Sian. . . Sian.' His voice was husky as he traced her throat with his open mouth, his breath hot against the sensitive skin.

She arched her neck breathlessly as shivers of arousal pierced her to the core. She loved the smooth, hard feel of his skin, the sweet, hot taste of his mouth.

Restlessly she moved her legs against the silky bed-spread, her body aching for him.

'Sam. . .please. . .' She arched her hips towards him, her legs parting helplessly as he slid one hand up the tender flesh of her inner thigh to reach the damp evidence of her arousal.

'Slowly, sweetheart,' he whispered against her lips, just before his tongue claimed her mouth in a sleek imitation of the way his fingers were claiming her body, seeking out the secret, sensitive places he once knew so well.

At the back of her mind, the small voice of her conscience was desperately trying to gain her attention, but when Sian felt his hardness pressing against her, nothing else mattered.

'Touch me,' he murmured hoarsely, and Sian's eyes were drawn down the length of his body, awed by the size and strength of his desire. His raw masculine beauty meant she needed no further urging to lower her hands and reach for him.

As their bodies met, Sian knew she wanted him, all of him, and she arched her back, thrusting her breasts up towards him, begging for his touch.

'Sam.' Her breath came in quick gasps as she cradled his head against her. 'Please. . .now. . .'

'Ah, Sian,' he breathed against her flesh, pausing for an age while she ached for his possession.

Finally he raised his head from its resting-place and met her eyes.

She knew.

As soon as she saw his expression, she knew with a

deep, hollow certainty what he was going to say. She closed her eyes tightly and wished that she could close her ears too, to that she wouldn't hear the words.

'We can't, can we?' he said softly, sadly. 'It wouldn't be right. Not when there's so much left to sort out, so much anger and bitterness left between us.'

Sian felt the blood leave her face as he spoke, the pain round her heart so deep she nearly moaned aloud. Then she remembered what she had said, what she had allowed him to do to her, what she had done in return, and she realised that she was still lying beneath him on the bed, her thighs cradling his hips, her arms around his shoulders. . .

The blush of mortification started at her breasts and travelled in a racing tide over her throat and face to her hairline. She turned her face to one side and tried to wrap her arms around herself to hide her shame, but he caught her wrists in his hands, then captured her chin and lifted it until she was forced to meet his gaze.

'No——' he shook his head '—you've got nothing to be ashamed about. . .'

She moaned wordlessly, her eyes filling with tears.

'Oh, sweetheart, I'm sorry.' He released her hands and used his thumbs to wipe away the tears gently. 'You'll never know what these moments in your arms have meant to me; how much I wanted to continue. . .'

'Then, why?' she wailed in misery. 'If you want to make love so much, why did you make me feel like. . . as if. . .' Two more tears rolled away from the corners of her eyes and into the hair at her temples.

'It's too soon. . .' His deep voice rumbled into the silence as she ran out of words. 'Until three days ago we hadn't seen each other for two years. . .'

'Does that matter?' Sian challenged. 'We still affect

each other the same way as when we first met, and it's not as if we're strangers.'

'Maybe that's why we should take things a little slower this time,' he said seriously. 'We made a mess of it last time.'

'Is there going to be a this time?' she asked in a small voice, her eyes gazing up at him wistfully.

'Who knows?' He shrugged, and the friction of the silky hair on his chest against her tender nipples reminded her of their intimate position.

'Sam?' She shifted slightly and he took her silent hint, sliding away from her just enough to relieve her of his weight before he captured her again in the tender warmth of his arms and cradled her head on his shoulder.

'We'll just have to take it a step at a time and see where it takes us,' he murmured into the softness of her hair, as she finally relaxed against him. 'Perhaps we'll finally get to see eye to eye. . .'

Sian's thoughts became muddled as sleep started to claim her. There was a niggling regret that she still hadn't told Sam what had really happened two years ago. She had been sidetracked by her explosive reaction to him.

Strange, she thought hazily. One minute she couldn't wait for him to make love to her, and the next, she was falling asleep in his arms. . .

Sian woke slowly and lay for a few minutes reliving the events of the past night. She was glad of the time to watch Sam as he slept, the way she had so many times when they were married. Soon he would wake and they would finally have to talk. . .

The telephone shrilled its summons.

'Yes?'

Sian smiled as she watched Sam reach out blindly, then mumble into the instrument.

His eyes were still tightly closed, his thick dark lashes forming shadowy crescents over his tanned cheekbones. His other arm was holding Sian's warm sleepy body firmly in position, sprawled across his chest, his hand hooked over the curve of her hip. His fingertips started describing tiny circles on her skin, arousing the nerves and sending a series of shivers up her spine and down to her toes.

'Sam? It's Philip.' The jovial voice boomed into the room as Sian lay contentedly watching Sam trying to wake up. His hair was tumbled on to his forehead and she reached up to run her fingers through the silky strands to smooth it back.

'What!'

Sam's eyes opened wide and he sat up suddenly, tipping her unceremoniously on to her back as he reached for his alarm clock.

'Damn.' He slammed it back down on the bedside cabinet. 'Thanks, Philip. Forgot to set the alarm last night,' and he dropped the receiver in position as he swung his legs over the side of the bed.

'Sian.' He reached across the rumpled bedding to smack her bare bottom. 'We didn't set the alarm last night. The bus leaves in fifteen minutes.'

'Oh, no!' She scrambled out of the other side of the bed to grab her clothes and realised that she hadn't left any ready. Last night she hadn't been in any fit state to remember to get her things ready for the morning.

She grabbed a plain white T-shirt and the only pair of jeans she had brought with her, and reached into the drawer for some underwear before she made for the bathroom.

Sam was just stepping out of the steam-filled shower as she walked in, and her heart started thudding against her ribs as she saw his lean, bronzed beauty before he wrapped a towel around himself.

As he turned towards the sink he caught sight of her standing in the doorway, and an expression of blatant hunger crossed his face.

'It's all yours,' he said in a husky voice.

His eyes travelled a heated path over her from head to toe and she suddenly realised that she was standing in front of him totally naked.

'It's all mine?' she queried softly as she approached him on silent bare feet, her heart suddenly light as air.

She slid one hand up over the damp swell of his chest muscles and along his shoulder. Curving her fingers around the back of his neck, she pulled his head down to touch her lips to his in a fleeting caress.

Before Sam could do more than open his mouth in invitation, she had danced back out of reach, depositing her clothes before she stepped blithely into the shower.

'No time for that this morning,' she admonished in a sing-song voice.

'Tease,' he growled, as he reached into the shower and ran one hand tantalisingly over her breast before tweaking her nipple. 'Just you wait. I'll find some way to get my revenge. . .'

Sian sagged against the cool tiled wall, her legs too shaky to hold her up as she watched Sam lather his face before starting to shave.

'Ten minutes left,' he reminded her, his eyes twinkling at her through the mirror as he watched her straighten away from the wall to shut the shower door.

They were ready with thirty seconds to spare, both

casting longing looks towards the dining-room on their way out.

'It's all your fault,' Sam grumbled, as they sped across the reception area towards the door. 'No meal last night and no breakfast this morning. . .'

Sian was too breathless to reply, saving her energy for worrying about the bad impression their poor timekeeping would make on the rest of the staff.

Philip met them just outside the doors with a cup of coffee for each of them and a couple of rolls.

'It's just cool enough to drink,' he advised. 'Knock it back and we'll be on our way.'

'Thanks, Philip,' Sian gasped. 'You're a life-saver,' and she downed the coffee in one go before climbing into the bus.

With the proximity of the other occupants of the bus there was no chance to talk, but Sian was content to sit close to Sam.

The silent journey became a pleasure when he captured her hand and held it pressed against his thigh, smiling down at her when she glanced at him, and giving her hand a gentle squeeze.

The first thing Sian noticed when they reached Orbis was the little figure huddled close to one of the plane's wheels.

'Sam——' she clutched his arm '—is that Chou? Over there by the wheel?'

She hurried up the bus, as soon as it came to a halt, and out on to the tarmac.

'Could you send the translator over, please?' she asked, as she sped over towards the shadowy area under the DC-10.

'Hi, Chou,' she called softly as she crouched down beside him.

The young child jerked in shock before slowly straightening up, his solemn face turning towards her.

Sian reached out to stroke one finger down the dried tearstains on his cheek.

'Hello, there.' She smiled, keeping her voice low. 'I wonder what happened to you yesterday. . .?'

The sound of footsteps behind her let her know the translator was coming, and she stood up and moved just far enough away to allow the young woman to crouch down beside Chou.

'Can you find out why he didn't come back yesterday?' Sian requested, hoping there hadn't been a worsening in the poor child's home circumstances.

'He says he was told to come back after the meal, but when he came everyone had gone.'

'But——'

'In his family, they eat one meal together. This is in the late afternoon.'

'So he came back this morning to find out where we had gone?' Sian couldn't help admiring his perseverance.

'No. He waited here all night to make sure you wouldn't take the plane away before you can look at his eyes.' The young woman looked up at her, her eyes becoming as tear-filled as Sian's.

'Will. . .?' Sian had to pause to clear her throat. 'Will you stay with him a minute while I find out what I can organise?'

The young woman smiled and nodded.

'I'll wait with him.'

Sian sped up the steps and into the plane, donning her disposable booties as automatically as if she had been working on Orbis for weeks.

'Joan?' She stuck her head round the corner and

called towards the sound of voices in the steriliser-room. 'Do you know where the medical director is?'

'Here.' The voice came from the communication centre behind her, right at the back of the plane, and made her jump.

'Chou is here,' Sian said in a breathless rush. 'There was a misunderstanding in the translation and he arrived after we went back to the hotel. He's been waiting under the plane all night so he wouldn't miss us. . .'

'Whoa. Slow down.' He held up one hand. 'Before you start trying to browbeat me again, you can do something useful instead. Go and collar whichever fellow is on the roster for the examination area and tell him I've given the go-ahead.'

Sian turned to make her way towards the front of the plane, but hadn't taken more than two steps before she whirled back, a huge smile lighting up her face.

'Thank you.' She clasped her hands together to contain her emotions, and drew in a deep breath. 'Thank you very much,' and she hurried forward again.

Five minutes later the interpreter was ushering Chou up the steps and leading him forward to the examination-room.

The Snellen alphabet chart with which Sian was so familiar in England had been replaced by a variation of the Rosenbaum screener, with representations of a capital E turned on its back, upside down and sideways in graduated sizes. It was a simple matter to ask patients, no matter what language they spoke and whether they were literate or not, to show which way the 'fingers' were pointing.

Next, Chou was settled on a chair in front of a frighteningly complicated piece of machinery.

'Can you explain to Chou that this machine won't

hurt him?' Frank asked the interpreter. 'It will just shine
a light into his eyes so I can see what has happened.' He
positioned the child's chin on the rest and pushed his
head forward gently until his forehead met the special
positioning bar.

Sian found herself surreptitiously crossing her fingers
as the tests continued, hoping that her initial diagnosis
would be borne out by this more detailed examination.

'Anterior chamber looks good. Nothing obviously
wrong with any of the structures behind the cornea and
lens, and the socket itself is completely normal,' Frank
reported at last. 'One eye is probably beyond help, but
the other one could be saved with a corneal graft.' He
turned to the interpreter and explained.

'The front layer of his eye has become clouded. If he
can have a window of clear membrane sewn in place of
his own membrane, then the light can get through and
he will be able to see properly again.'

'What are the chances of getting a cornea today?' Sian
asked in a taut voice, her hands clenched tightly into
fists as she waited for his reply.

'Not good.' Frank pulled a face.

'But there are two eye banks in Beijing. Surely——'

'It's a matter of setting it all up and getting the co-
ordination just right.'

'There must be some way to do it.' Frustration filled
her voice. 'How do we get things moving?'

'That's the medical director's privilege. He and Celia
regularly move mountains, between them.' He smiled at
her, and smoothed his hand over Chou's head. 'Take
this young man with you when you ask. I'm sure he's no
more immune than any man to a beautiful, determined
woman and a helpless child!'

'If only life really was that simple,' Sian quipped, as

she settled Chou in one of the chairs and set off on the next stage of her self-appointed task.

'I'm sorry.' The medical director shook his head. 'There's very little chance of getting a cornea today, even if we had time to do the operation.'

'What about tomorrow?' she pleaded.

'We've already got a full programme booked tomorrow, too. Everyone will be too tired at the end of the week to want to stay on for an extra hour or more.'

'But it would be possible to get a donor cornea if you approached the two eye banks in Beijing?' Sian prompted hopefully.

'It's possible. . .' he conceded.

'So if I offered to pay for the extra fuel to keep Orbis running for that much longer tomorrow afternoon——'

'Have you any idea how much that would cost?' he interrupted. 'Orbis uses about a thousand gallons of fuel a day when she's on the ground.'

'How can you put a price on a child's sight?' she countered quietly. 'I'm only too willing to pay.'

'Even so. . .'

'And if I can find enough staff to volunteer to man the operating-room for the surgery——'

'All right.' He sounded resigned. 'I'll see what I can do but I'm not promising anything. You just make sure you don't get your hopes up too high.'

Sian's mood was buoyant for the rest of the morning as she planned which members of the team to approach first.

'I should go for the ones who have had most rest in the afternoon,' Joan advised. 'You're operating in the morning and you haven't got a lecture scheduled, so you should be fresh. Now you just need to look at the roster to eliminate those due to take the last shift that afternoon.'

'Thanks, Joan.' Sian blew a kiss in her direction. 'You're a mine of information.'

It was while she was waiting to speak to the nurse-anaesthetist that Sam approached her in the corridor.

'I need to speak to you,' he murmured, obviously conscious that they could have company at any moment.

'Is it about tomorrow afternoon?' she prompted, her mind full of her hopes for Chou's surgery.

'No. It's about last night. . .'

He paused as Sians's eyes widened, surprised that he should bring their private life up like this.

'What. . .?'

'After what happened—nearly hapened——' he was avoiding her startled gaze, his eyes flickering anywhere but at her '—it's just. . .until we've. . . We can't afford to take any risks over. . . You *are* protected, aren't you?' he muttered.

If he had been watching, he would have seen her shocked response. As it was, he took the sound as confirmation.

'I thought you would be,' he said flatly. 'You made certain of it while we were married. . .'

'Until the dentist put me on antibiotics,' she reminded him sharply.

'Yes. Well. . .we all know what happened then——'

'Do we?' She cut across his words pointedly. '*I* know what happened, but you never bothered to ask. You just assumed you knew without even talking to me.'

She bit her lip, conscious that her voice had risen from the discreet murmur they had been using.

'In that case, if you feel so strongly about it, it's time we sat down and thrashed the whole thing out once and for all.' He drew himself up to his full height and pulled his shoulders back before he continued. 'I've got an hour or so free this afternoon after the cataract surgery. I suggest we meet outside.'

'Fine,' she agreed dully. 'I'll see you then.'

Sian watched him stride away towards the front of the plane, and her heart ached. She knew that they needed to talk but she also knew how much it would hurt both of them to open old wounds.

Suddenly she remembered his reason for speaking to her just now, and her hands clenched into tight fists as her anger grew.

How dared he presume that he had the right to ask her such questions?

Her shock at hearing him ask if she was protected against pregnancy had left her lost for words, the hurt compounded when he had thrown at her the events leading up to the end of their marriage.

Now she had the prospect of an acrimonious discussion of the events leading up to their divorce to look forward to.

There was no way she was going to tell him that she hadn't been using a contraceptive for two years. That, once they had separated, there had been no point in taking anything as she had no intention of making love—how could she when Sam still held her heart?

Sian was waiting nervously for Sam to finish inserting the final stitches after a successful cataract removal when Joan called her.

'Have you got a couple of minutes free?' She was using her best wheedling tone.

'All right, Joan. I'll bite. What do you want?'

'Could you go outside and get some stores from

underneath the plane? We need some more sterile water and some more four-oh silk sutures.'

'OK. Where do I get them?' Sian bent down to remove her booties, glad for something to do to take her mind off the coming meeting with Sam.

'You'll need these.' Joan handed her ear protectors. 'And you'll need to go up the ladder into both storage areas. The sterile water bottles are packed in cardboard boxes with a large stencil on the outside, and they're just inside the front opening on the left. The needles are——'

'I remember where they are, from last time I went.' She smiled. 'By the time I leave, I should just about know my way around well enough to be useful.'

It was hot outside, the sun beating relentlessly down on the runway, which reflected it straight back.

The ladder was already hooked to the front storage area opening, and Sian made a couple of journeys up into the belly of the plane to carry down the sterile water. Then she unhooked the ladder from the rail just inside the front opening and walked back to put it in position in the second opening.

'Right first time,' she murmured as she reached for the four-oh silk, her voice all but inaudible over the sound of the generator.

She turned to descend the ladder, feeling carefully over the edge with her foot for the first rung.

It wasn't there.

She stretched her foot out further behind her.

Still no ladder.

Finally, she peered out of the opening and saw the familiar shape lying on the ground in the shadow underneath Orbis.

'Oh, no,' she groaned, as she remembered the

horror stories the permanent staff had told the visitors about the times the ladder had blown down on the old DC-8.

She ran her fingers along the specially designed rail. The ladder on the DC-10 was designed to clip on to the rail so that it couldn't blow down while someone was in the storage area.

Except, I seem to have managed it. I can't have hooked it on properly, she said to herself disgustedly. I'm the only one out here and it's too far to jump. Even if I shout, no one will hear me with the generator going. Perhaps I'll be able to attract someone's attention when they come down the steps. . .

She lay face down, her head over the opening to wait for a rescuer to appear.

Sam should be out of OR soon, she reminded herself, the heat assailing her as it was reflected upwards from the surrounding tarmac. He'll come looking for me in a minute. . .

She composed herself to wait patiently in spite of her discomfort.

It wasn't very long before her head started to pound, and Sian remembered that she had intended getting herself a can of drink.

I'd be all right if this had happened in the other hold. I could have had some of the sterile water. . .

She rested her aching head on her arm and closed her eyes against the reflected glare.

'Oh, Lord. I hope Sam doesn't think I'm trying to avoid him. . .' Her voice was insignificant against the surrounding noise.

'Sian?'

A voice was calling her, but it couldn't be important because they weren't shouting very loud, and it was just too much effort to lift her head to see what they wanted, anyway. . .

It was so hot. . .and she was so thirsty. . .and her eyes were so heavy. . .

CHAPTER SEVEN

'Sian.'

Sam's voice sounded so close, but she didn't seem to be able to open her eyes.

A cool cloth was smoothed over her forehead and she murmured her grateful approval.

''s nice.' She tilted her face up to allow the blessed coolness to travel down her throat and round under her hair.

'Can you take a sip of this?' Sam's voice urged, as a hand supported the back of her head and a straw touched her lips.

The liquid flowing into her parched throat tasted like nectar. She was so thirsty. . .

'Slowly.' The straw was withdrawn before she had a chance to quench her thirst, and she screwed her face up in disappointment.

'More,' she demanded petulantly.

'In a minute.' She heard the chuckle in his voice and forced one eye open to fix him with a glare.

'I'm still thirsty,' she pronounced with exaggerated emphasis.

'You'll be all right in a minute,' he promised, and she saw a strange expression cross his face before he leant down to press a gentle kiss on her forehead. 'I'm sorry, sweetheart,' he murmured softly.

'What for?' Sian managed to open both eyes, and glanced past one broad shoulder clad in pale blue short-sleeved scrubs. It took several seconds before she recognised the recovery-room towards the rear of Orbis. 'What am I doing in here?'

'Recovering,' he said drily.

'From what?'

'You passed out in the storage hold. . .'

'Oh. . .' Suddenly it all came back to her. 'I remember, now. . . The ladder fell down and I couldn't jump out and no one came. . . It was so hot. . .'

'I'm sorry.' His hand squeezed hers convulsively and she realised he must have been holding it for some time.

'Why?' She was puzzled. 'It wasn't *your* fault. I can't have attached the ladder properly when I went into the hold.'

'I should have come looking for you,' he insisted harshly. 'I should have known. . .'

'You *couldn't* have known it would happen,' Sian objected, her innate honesty making her add, 'It was my own fault for not checking.'

'I should have realised there was something wrong when you didn't turn up for our talk,' he said in a low voice. 'Instead, I thought you were avoiding me and. . .' He lifted his shoulders in a wry shrug.

'You left me to my own devices and went to have some lunch,' she guessed—accurately, if the sweep of colour over his cheekbones was anything to go by.

She captured the straw to drink again, this time pulling a face at the taste of the salt and sugar mixed in the water to speed her recovery. 'How long was I in there?'

'Over an hour during the hottest part of the day, as far as we can tell. It wasn't until Philip needed some four-oh silk that Joan realised you hadn't brought any back with you.'

'What happened to the sterile water?' She suddenly remembered the other part of her task.

'One of the flight mechanics saw it on the ground and carried it in. Joan thought he was just helping you out.'

'So how did I get here?' she wondered aloud.

'I carried you.' His eyes met hers full-on for the first time since she'd woken, and she saw the anguish in them. 'I caught sight of your arm hanging out of the rear opening and. . .' He lifted her hand. The contrast between its slender paleness and the tanned strength of his had never seemed so obvious before.

'God!' The word exploded out of him. 'I thought you were dead. . .' and he buried his lips in her soft palm.

'Sam?'

Philip's voice came through to them from the lockers round the corner.

'Yeah?' Sam's voice sounded hoarse.

'Your patient will be coming through for prepping in about five minutes.' He stuck his head round, a concerned expression on his face. 'Are you going to be OK, or do you want me to take it?'

Sam sat very still, his eyes fixed fiercely on Sian's face while he drew in a deep breath and released it slowly.

'Thanks, but I'll be fine.' He smiled rather wearily. 'I'll be ready by the time the patient is.'

Sian was the forgotten spectator to the exchange and marvelled at the metamorphosis she saw take place in Sam.

In the space of a minute he had gone from being an overwrought man to a self-controlled, highly trained surgeon.

Watching the change take place reminded Sian of the two very different sides which went to make up the man she loved.

Unfortunately, two years ago they had both lost sight of the difficulties which this created: the internal battles which he sometimes had to fight to rationalise the two sides of his nature.

'Will you be all right?' He squeezed her hand, then released it gently. 'I need to go and scrub up in a minute.'

'Don't worry about me.' She patted his arm. 'I'll have a ringside seat while you're operating and afterwards you can take me to dinner.'

'Right.' He smiled. 'Keep sipping. It might not be a gin and tonic but it's probably doing you more good,' and he disappeared through the doors separating the recovery area from the instrument-room and the scrub-room.

It wasn't long before the operating-room 'went live', as Sam prefaced the operation with a short explanation.

'This gentleman is approximately fifty years old and, as you can see from the whitish opacity of his lens, he has cataracts. The grounds for their removal are individual to each case—for example, a visual acuity of twenty over seventy or worse, due to cataracts, is usually judged as grounds for cataract removal, but an elderly illiterate person may get along quite well with twenty over two hundred vision.'

He paused for a moment to allow the translators to catch up before he made his next point.

'In this case, the gentleman's acuity is relatively good at twenty over forty, but he works as a watchmaker and repairer of fine ophthalmic surgical instruments and machinery. . .'

He paused, knowing that his audience would see the humour in the situation. Sam would be preserving the sight of someone who would be helping, in his own way, to save the sight of others.

'Most cataract surgery,' he continued calmly, 'is

performed under local anaesthetic with injections used for local nerve-blocking to prevent movement of the eye during surgery.

'Usually, the eye is opened through an incision around the top of the cornea and a narrow freezing-probe is introduced. This sticks to the lens as it freezes it, so that the lens can be peeled away and pulled out. The cornea is then sutured closed.'

'He makes it sound so perfectly simple, doesn't he?' Liz commented, as she perched beside Sian to watch on the monitor.

'Mmm,' Sian agreed wordlessly, too wrapped up in Sam's presentation to bother with conversation.

'The method I'll be demonstrating now is removal of the lens with a phacoemulsifier.' He held the instrument so that it was visible to the camera.

'This is a narrow, ultravibratory instrument which breaks up the opaque lens into tiny fragments which are then suctioned out.'

Again, he paused for a moment before continuing, his pacing calm and deliberate.

'One of the benefits of this method is that the incision can be much smaller, as the lens is not removed as a whole. Another benefit is the wider range of replacement lens implants which can be used.'

Once again, Sam directed the camera towards the subject of his talk, this time a selection of lens implants which were designed to be inserted in the eye in the place of the lens being removed.

The procedure began, with Sam talking his audience carefully through each stage.

At intervals he also digressed into side issues, such as the possible complications of cataract surgery in general and the emulsification procedure in particular.

'It is essential that the surgeon is well skilled in the technique before he attempts to use it, especially in his control of the phacoemulsifier, as it must be applied only to the lens. . .'

The operation and its subsequent discussion lasted for more than an hour, with questions coming thick and fast from both the class-room at the front of the plane and the other packed class-room in one of the airport buildings.

As ever, Sian was riveted by Sam's mastery of his chosen field, and her heart was filled with pride.

The more she saw of him, the more she regretted their divorce. She had the utmost respect for him as a first-class surgeon and she loved him so much. . .

'Right!' The object of her thoughts came through into the recovery-room to check his patient over quickly, then turned to Sian, stripping off his disposable cap and reaching for the ties on his gown. 'Nearly time to go back to the hotel' He rubbed his hands together in anticipation.

'Not until clean-up's finished,' Sian reminded him, and laughed at the face he pulled. 'Go on, Cinderella. Get back to that sink and get scrubbing!'

'Cinderella?' he growled. 'It's lucky for you that you're still looking pale or I'd make you pay for that.' He faked a swipe at her as he went past on the way to the operating-room.

'Don't forget your bucket and mop. . .' she called after him, her heart buoyant inside her.

There was definitely a new feeling of ease between the two of them since her mishap in the hold this afternoon.

Sian hugged herself.

Being stranded had been frightening as well as potentially dangerous, especially as she hadn't drunk enough fluids during the morning to combat the effects of the heat. In spite of that, it would have been a blessing in disguise if it had finally helped Sam to realise the depth of his feelings for her.

Now, she just had to wait until they returned to the hotel before they were able really to talk to each other

Sam insisted that Sian should take it easy when they finally reached their room, suggesting that she took a quick shower while he ordered some food to be delivered to the room.

She floated happily into the bathroom, basking in the delights of being pampered and cared for.

One look in the mirror made her squeak in horror.

She hadn't realised what a mess she looked, her hair limp and sweat-matted and her face streaked with dust from the hold.

A vigorous shower and shampoo restored her cleanliness, and an application of her favourite moisturiser completed the ritual. It was so warm that her hair needed little more than a thorough towelling to be dry, and she was left with just one decision to make — whether to go out to the room with a towel wrapped around her, or to don the fine cotton nightdress she had brought with her into the bathroom, or to wear nothing at all. . .

Cowardice won in the end, and she slipped the nightdress over her head and smoothed it into position. It was white in a fine nainsook cotton with spaghetti straps which tied at the shoulder. It reached to just below mid-thigh, leaving a long length of slender leg on show.

She cast one last look at herself in the mirror, running her fingers through her hair to fluff it up a little and childishly sticking her tongue out at herself before she turned to open the door.

The room was empty.

'So much for my grand entrance,' she muttered, then thanked her lucky stars she had decided to put something on when she saw the tray of covered dishes waiting for her. 'What if the waiter had been out here when I opened he door. . .' She didn't know whether to laugh or blush at the thought.

But where was Sam? Why wasn't he here?

She sat down to lift the covers off the plates and her heart sank. The lingering hope that he was going to be joining her for her meal died. This was definitely a meal intended for one.

The meal should have been delicious—the food in the hotel was superb—but her thoughts were elsewhere as she doggedly ate the dishes Sam had ordered for her. It was hardest when she was eating the fresh lychees he had chosen for her dessert. Had he remembered that they were a special favorite of hers?

It wasn't until she set the tray outside the door that her fighting spirit started to surface again.

'I'll be blowed if I'll just tuck myself into bed and go off to sleep like a good little girl,' she declared to the empty room.

She picked up the novel she had started on the journey out to Beijing, and settled herself against the mound of pillows on her bed, reaching across to borrow Sam's before she was comfortable.

'Right, Sam Forrester.' She flicked through the pages, looking for her marker. 'You might have decided to put off the evil hour by taking yourself off until I go to sleep, but you're in for a big surprise. We're going to have that talk whether you like it or not.'

In spite of the warmth of the room she gave a little shiver of apprehension. She was dreading it, but she was also longing for the confrontation to be over so that they could go on to more important matters.

Sian gave herself a mental shake. There was no point in getting ahead of herself. Concentrate on one thing at a time. She looked down at her book, focusing determinedly on the words until at last she became engrossed in the story.

Her eyelids were just starting to feel heavy when she heard the key being slipped gently into the lock and she looked up just in time to see the handle turn.

If she had been in a light-hearted mood the expression of shock on Sam's face would have made her laugh aloud.

'Hello, Sam.' She smiled calmly in spite of the tattoo her heart was beating out on her ribs. 'I wondered how long it would be before you came back.'

She watched as he came into the room, his jacket hung over his shoulder from one finger, his short-sleeved shirt opened at the neck to reveal a V of golden tanned skin overlaid with dark swirls of hair.

He went across to the wardrobe and hung his jacket away neatly before speaking.

'I thought you'd be asleep by now,' he said quietly, his back remaining towards her as he walked towards the bathroom, pulling his shirt-tails free from the waistband of his trousers as he went.

'Don't you mean you *hoped* I'd be asleep by now?' she retorted crisply. 'I'm surprised at you. I didn't think you were a coward.'

There was a measure of grim satisfaction when she saw his shoulders stiffen at the gibe, and he slowly turned towards her, his face coldly furious.

'Of course, it wouldn't occur to you that I was being considerate. That I thought you needed a bit of peace and quiet and an early night after your mishap this afternoon.'

'I'm not made of porcelain,' she objected swiftly. 'And if I did feel the need for seclusion I think I'm quite capable of asking for it. Obviously it's a lot easier to come by than congenial company.'

'That's another reason why I left you alone.' He stood in the doorway to the bathroom, the fist he planted on each hip pulling the unbuttoned edges of his shirt apart to reveal the dark hair arrowing into the waistband of his trousers.

Sian was distracted by the sight, losing the thread of the conversation for a moment while her eyes traced the extent of naked body displayed by his position.

'Don't.' His voice was low and husky and recalled her attention, her brow furrowing briefly.

'What?' She was puzzled, her eyes wide as she looked up at him.

He took a step towards her and stopped, clenching his hands into fists and releasing them again.

'Don't look at me like that, or all that time I spent walking around the hotel grounds will have been wasted.'

She saw him draw in a deep breath, his chest expanding deeply before he shook his head. 'It's pretty hopeless, really. . .' His words trailed away and her heart sank at the implications.

Sian leant weakly back against the pile of pillows, her heart in her throat and a sick feeling deep inside.

She had thought that their new harmony would ease the way for their talk, but Sam seemed to have decided otherwise. She closed her eyes as despair swept over her.

'Sian?' She heard the soft brush of his feet on the deep-pile carpet as he approached her, and steeled herself to control her emotions before she opened her eyes to look up at him.

'Are you feeling all right?' He sat down on the side of the bed, his weight on the mattress tilting her towards him. She put out a hand to steady herself and he captured it, his lean fingers circling her wrist to feel for her pulse.

She was tempted to take her arm away but the contact, no matter how professionally directed, was balm to her disappointment. He seemed so caring, so concerned for her welfare. If only he cared as much for her emotions. . .

'I was thinking. . .' His words emerged as a low rumble. 'While I was walking, I was thinking about my feelings when I thought you were ducking out on our talk. . .' He put up one hand to halt her attempted interruption. 'Now I know that you weren't avoiding me, but at the time. . .' He raised his dark lashes and fixed her with his gaze. 'I was hurt,' he finished simply.

'Hurt pride?' she prompted quietly, realising that this was her chance to find out his real feelings about their situation.

'Some, certainly,' he admitted. 'I was blaming you for leaving me in the dark about your motives, but it wasn't until I found out what had really happened—that you were trapped in the hold while I was cursing at you— that I realised I was repeating history.'

'I don't understand. What history?'

'It was something you said on the plane this morning. You said that you knew what happened two years ago but I never even asked you to tell me. I just assumed that I knew—and this evening I realised that I had been doing it again. I presumed that you were avoiding me because you didn't meet me as we had arranged.'

'In the circumstances, it might have been logical. . .'

'No. I should have confronted you and asked you face to face. If I had, you'd have been found so much sooner. . .'

'So this is an attack of guilt, is it?' She sat up a little straighter. 'Will it make you feel better if I grant you absolution. . .if I say I forgive you for thinking the worst of me? What about two years ago? Will that come under the same amnesty?'

'Now, wait a minute.' His jaw squared and his gaze became suddenly cooler. 'Two years ago we were married, we were fully qualified ophthalmologists and you were expecting my baby——'

'*Our* baby,' she broke in, her voice husky with remembered pain. 'She was my baby, too. . .' Her throat closed over the words and she could feel the burning pressure of tears behind her eyes.

'Yes. Our baby,' he conceded coldly. 'The baby you didn't want because you had a chance at a prestigious new job. A real giant's step up the promotion ladder.'

'We hadn't planned to start a family. . .' Her voice came out thin and reedy as she remembered the events.

'I know we hadn't planned it. It was the antibiotics the dentist gave you without telling you they would stop your pill working, but. . .' He raked the fingers of both hands through his hair, leaving it standing on end.

'Why did you get rid of it?' The words exploded out of him as if they had been dammed up inside him under terrible pressure.

'We could have managed,' he pleaded, his eyes filled with a dreadful wild agony. 'You didn't have to kill our baby to have your career!'

He leapt up from the side of the bed and started pacing furiously from one end of the room to the other, and it was only the desolate expression on his face and in his dark, liquid eyes that prevented her from physically attacking him for his unjust words.

'Who told you I killed it?' Her words were softly spoken but had the impact of a shout.

Instantly, he halted in his tracks and whirled to face her.

'Who told me?' he repeated, as if she wasn't quite sane. 'No one *told* me. No one else knew you were pregnant until you weren't. . .'

'So how did you know what had happened to the baby?' she persisted. 'You were away for three days in Birmingham at that conference.'

It was costing her dearly to remain outwardly calm, her heart beating frantically and her body consumed by a fine tremor.

'I arrived back at the flat and you weren't there.' His eyes were focused on his memories. 'Mrs Simpson heard me clattering about in the kitchen. . .' His voice dropped slightly and his cheeks coloured. 'I was cooking a meal so it would be ready when you came home. . .'

'Oh, Sam,' she breathed.

'She knocked on the door and told me you probably wouldn't be home till the next day.' He grimaced. 'The conversation was a bit surreal for a few minutes, with her saying you were *in* the hospital and me thinking she meant *at*, and wondering how she knew your timetable better than I did.'

He gave a tired smile and walked slowly across to sit on the edge of his own bed, hunching forward to rest his elbows on his knees, his hands dangling limply between them.

'By the time I got to the hospital I was panicking. I had no idea what was wrong, even what floor to look for you. I must have looked like a wild man when I got to Obs and Gyn.' He lifted his downbent head to gaze straight at her before he said his final words. 'That's where I was told what you'd done.'

The silence stretched into infinity before Sian ventured a question.

'Who told you?' she demanded quietly. 'What exactly did they say?'

'Oh, for heaven's sake. . .'

'No, Sam,' she said, as firmly as her quavering voice would allow. 'I listened to you and now I need to ask some questions. What did they say—*exactly*?' she stressed the final word.

'God.' He raked his fingers through his hair again. 'You should have been a lawyer.' He threw both hands up in the air. 'How can I remember the exact words? It's two years ago. All I can remember clearly is Sister taking me into her office. I thought she was going to tell me you were desperately ill. When I heard her say you'd had an abortion I must have gone into shock.' He dropped his face into his hands.

'I miscarried, Sam.'

'What?' The word was muffled until he raised his head sharply.

'It was a spontaneous abortion. A miscarriage. . .' and before she could control them the tears started to trickle down her cheeks as she started to sob. 'I lost our b-baby and you made me feel so g-guilty. . .' She rolled away from him and buried her face in the pillows to hide her escalating grief.

She felt the mattress dip as he joined her on the bed,

but it was long tear-racked moments before she felt the solid warmth of his arm surround her shoulders.

'Shh,' he whispered against her hair, as he turned her into his arms and cradled her against the sheltering strength of his broad chest. 'Hush, now. No more. . .' One hand pulled her head into the curve of his jaw and they fitted together like interlocking parts of a puzzle. 'You'll drown us both if you keep this up. . .'

It was a weak attempt at humour and neither of them laughed, but it seemed to slow the flood of tears.

For a long time they sat together, Sian cradled on Sam's lap, her breathing hitching every so often as she recovered from her tears.

'I've cried more in the last twenty-four hours than I have in——' She managed to stop just in time, but the words were hovering in the air as though she had said them aloud.

'Why didn't you *tell* me?' The impassioned words were spoken against the crown of her head, their force stirring her hair and warming her scalp with his breath.

'How?' she said flatly. 'When? Before you exploded or after you had branded me a selfish, self-centred murderer?'

'I asked you whether you'd done it deliberately but you never answered. You never told me how it happened. . .'

'I did a lot of thinking while you were away at that conference—about our individual ambitions and our goals as a couple. I know we hadn't intended starting a family so soon. We hadn't really discussed that side of things much—we were both working so hard at our jobs.'

'But didn't you realise——?'

'Please.' She lifted her head from its secure niche and

begged him with her eyes. 'Please, let me get this out in my own way. . .'

His eyes darkened as he gazed down at her, but he nodded and gently returned her head to its resting-place, his hand remaining to stroke the silky curls.

'The funny thing was, the more I thought about having our baby, the more I liked the idea. But I didn't know what you really thought about it—whether we could cope financially if we lost my income, whether our marriage could stand the stress of a baby so soon. We'd had so little time to be a couple and already we were going to be a family. . .'

She drew in a deep shuddering breath, knowing that the worst part was still to come.

'I was waiting for you to come back so we could talk about our choices. If you thought we could manage, I would postpone my career until the baby was school-age, then perhaps return part-time, even though it would affect my prospects.

'What I was hoping was that I could persuade you to let me continue working as long as I could manage to keep on top of everything.'

'So what went wrong?' She was grateful to realise that the soft words were more of an encouragement to continue than an accusation.

'I did too much,' she said simply, and waited.

'Too much of what?'

'I suppose you'd call it spring-cleaning for want of a better term—after all, it was July. By the time I realised the backache wasn't just from re-hanging the curtains, it was too late.'

'I still don't understand why you didn't tell me. You've never been shy of telling me where to get off before. Why this time?'

She was silent for a long time before she could form the words which would expose her darkest secret.

'When you accused me of getting rid of the baby on purpose, I suddenly wondered if it was true. Had it been a subconscious desire to get rid of the baby that made me do too much. . .?' Her throat closed and her shoulders shook with renewed tears.

'I had no idea. No idea at all.' He rocked her as if she was the baby, gently swaying backwards and forwards. 'One minute you were applying for a prestigious post, the next you realised you were pregnant, then you weren't pregnant any more and you were taking up your new post. It all seemed so cut and dried, especially as you never denied anything. . .'

'I didn't think I should *have* to defend myself,' she said, her voice nearly under control again. 'I loved you and you said you loved me. I thought that meant we trusted each other but——' she shrugged '—perhaps we didn't know each other as well as we thought. Perhaps it was a mistake to get married in the first place. . .'

Sian's heart ached as she waited to hear Sam deny her words, and her hopes sank into oblivion when he remained silent.

Suddenly everything caught up with her, and she ran out of even enough energy to keep her eyes open.

Slowly she relaxed, curving bonelessly against the breadth of Sam's chest and the strength of his encircling arms, surrounded by an aura of safety and comfort.

The last thing she remembered was Sam's gentle kiss on her forehead, and she made a half-hearted attempt to return the gesture before sleep claimed her.

CHAPTER EIGHT

As SHE started to surface from sleep, Sian was aware of a strange sensation. It felt as if she was surrounded, and she wondered sleepily if the nightmare had taken a new twist.

She still had the same feeling that Sam was somehow involved, just as in the other awful dreams, but this time. . .

'Are you awake?'

The deep murmur right beside her ear made her eyes fly open and she turned her head—to gaze straight into Sam's sleepy eyes.

'Sam!' Her heart gave a nervous little skip. 'Have— have you been there all night?' She felt her cheeks heating in a crazy blush.

'I had to,' he said seriously, his eyes darkly mournful. 'You wouldn't let go of me.'

'Ha!' Sian fought the temptation to laugh. 'Unlikely!' She drew back the covers far enough to reveal one of his darkly furred forearms resting almost possessively across her waist. 'Who's holding whom, here?'

She smiled victoriously up at him and watched his eyes darken as the pupils dilated, his gaze fixed on the shadows of her breasts faintly visible through the fine fabric of her nightdress.

As they watched, her nipples tightened, jutting proudly in a shameless invitation to his touch.

Sian held her breath, waiting to see what Sam would

135

do. His burgeoning arousal against her thigh was something neither of them could deny, but. . .

He paused, one finger poised to accept her body's plea.

'Dammit!' He swore and rolled away from her, climbing out of bed to silence the alarm clock ringing insistently on the other side of his own bed.

He sat down on the rumpled covers with his back towards her, and braced his elbows on his knees before he dropped his head into his hands and scrubbed his palms over his stubbly cheeks.

If she'd had any doubts about it, her brief glimpse of Sam as he'd reached for the alarm clock had confirmed the fact that he was totally, unashamedly naked.

She gazed longingly at the firm golden skin, the bars of early morning sunlight flooding over him tantalising her to touch, to explore. The taut width of his shoulders, the muscles more defined than when they had been married, the long, lean length of his back and his tight, rounded buttocks, several shades paler than the rest. All of it, just the sight of it, made her palms itch with the need to stroke, to trace each muscle, to. . .

'I can feel your eyes on me.' Sam's voice was husky in the silence. 'They make me feel as if my skin's on fire, as if I'm burning up inside. . .' He turned slightly, just twisting his shoulders so that their eyes met in a soul-deep recognition that could have lasted a fraction of a second or a thousand years.

Finally, the sounds of the other hotel guests intruded, voices outside the door recalling them to the present.

'Where do we go from here?' Sian asked softly.

She knew, as she had always known deep in her heart, that Sam was her first and last love—her only love. The commitment and passion she had always felt for him had grown even stronger, now that she knew how empty her life was without him.

Her question had made Sam tense. His shoulders rising almost imperceptibly as he thought what to say.

'We need to think,' he said cautiously, and Sian could have wept. Where was the fiery man who had swept her off her feet? Had their terrible misunderstanding had such a drastic effect on his whole character?

She slid out of the other side of the bed, grateful for the covering of her nightdress as she made her way towards the bathroom.

'I'm first in the operating-room this morning,' she said quietly, hiding her sadness under the ordinary day-to-day necessities. 'There isn't really time to start talking about——'

'Lunchtime,' he broke in, rising to his full height and stepping into her path with a supple stride. 'Today's Friday—the last day on Orbis. We'll all be gone by tomorrow and the next team flies in on Sunday.'

He reached out to take one tightly fisted hand in his and uncurl the fingers gently before dropping a fleeting kiss in her palm. 'Talk to me at lunchtime?'

She was desperate for every last minute he would allow her, but her pride prevented her from agreeing too easily. She knew how *she* felt, but he still hadn't told her his feelings.

'If I don't get trapped in the storage hold again,' she said lightly, smiling up at his watchful face when she saw it crease into answering humour.

'At least I'd know enough to come looking for you this time.' He tapped her familiarly on her bottom to hurry her towards the bathroom, his warm hand lingering slightly longer than necessary. 'Have your shower, woman. I've no intention of missing my breaskfast this morning.'

Sian's first question when she saw the medical director was about the cornea for Chou.

'Any news from the eye banks?' She buttonholed him as soon as he came in to the dining-room.

'Nothing, so far. But apparently there was some further coverage in the papers this morning about Orbis and the accord we signed with China. The eye banks came in for a lot of praise, so hopefully this will put them on their mettle.'

Sian crossed her fingers and held them up for him to see.

'You won't be able to operate like that,' he teased. 'You'll have to cross them mentally.'

'You will let me know as soon as you hear anything. . .?'

'I promise, you'll be the first to know.'

It nearly broke Sian's heart when the first person she saw when they arrived at the plane was Chou.

She and the interpreter hurried across to him together.

'He hasn't been here all night, I hope,' Sian muttered, as they reached the shadows under Orbis.

It wasn't until the interpreter started speaking that Sian realised that there was another figure beside Chou—an elderly man who stood politely when he realised they had visitors.

'This gentleman is Chou's grandfather. He has come to wait with Chou.'

Sian reached out to take the elderly man's hand and press it between her own.

'Will you tell him he is very welcome to wait, but we don't know how long it will be?'

The interpreter conducted a short conversation in the strangely liquid-sounding language before she reported back to Sian.

'He says that the wait will not seem long if you can do something for his grandson.'

Sian squeezed his hand again, and hoped with all her heart that she wouldn't have to disappoint Chou's grandfather.

If the cornea arrived in time she was confident that the keratoplasty operation would be a success. The option if it didn't arrive in time was something she was trying to shut out of her mind.

'It is going to be very difficult for Chou. Because we don't know what time his operation is, he mustn't have anything to eat today,' she warned.

'I will tell his grandfather this,' the young Chinese woman confirmed with a smile.

'Will you explain that I must go now to get ready for the operations this morning?' Sian requested, before she hurried towards the steps and started to compose herself for the surgery she had scheduled first thing this morning.

Now that she knew the routine on Orbis, it didn't take long before she was scrubbed, gowned and gloved and sitting in position at the operating microscope.

'Good-morning, ladies and gentlemen.' Sian knew that her voice was much steadier than it had been for her first 'live' operation, but she still noticed the effects of adrenalin when the message 'ready to go live' went out.

'Our patient today is a two-year-old boy with lamellar cataract.' She paused, copying Sam's method of pacing to allow the interpreter time to deal with technical terms.

'This is a disc-shaped opacity within the lens, a bit like a tiny plate. It usually has a thickened rim which is generally concealed by the edge of the pupil.

'It is a congenital condition,' she continued, 'and is often the result of lowered blood calcium just before or after the birth of the baby.'

Sian knew of the programmes Orbis International was helping to organise in various countries around the world. Knowing the importance of this assistance in the early detection of visual impairment, Sian took the opportunity to stress the point.

'Cataracts in young children are detected by looking at the red reflex, and this should be a routine part of the examination of a young child. If there is any doubt, they should be referred immediately, especially if both eyes are affected.'

She waited for a minute before she continued.

'Binocular congenital cataracts should be cleared within a few months of the birth of the child. It is only safe to delay any longer when only one eye is involved, as with our patient today.'

Her host ophthalmologist this time was one of the small but growing number of female eye-surgeons in China. Although Sian knew that each of the host surgeons who assisted in the operations on Orbis had been carefully chosen, this one in particular proved to be excellent.

By the time the operation ended, she knew that it had been a perfect text-book procedure for the library of edited tapes Orbis would be leaving behind when she went on to her next mission.

Afterwards, Sian felt that it was a shame that the two

of them had no language in common, because she would have loved to discuss the many similarities and differences they could have discovered between their training and ideologies, especially in view of their gender.

As it was, they were limited to smiles and translations and she was left with a lingering feeling of frustration.

As she made her way back through the recovery-room, she saw the medical director's back disappearing into the communication centre and hurried after him.

'Excuse me.' She stuck her head round the entrance and was greeted by a raised hand as he held a telephone to his ear.

She waited, almost hopping from one foot to the other in her impatience.

Two large hands descended on her shoulders.

She tilted her head back to see who was holding her, but she needn't have bothered. She would know Sam's touch anywhere.

'Any news yet?' he murmured. 'I take it you're waiting to hear about Chou's cornea?'

'That's right, but no news yet.' She held up her crossed fingers. 'I'm hoping that's what the phone call is about.'

As she said the words, the medical director turned towards them shaking his head.

Sian's shoulders slumped in spite of the fact that Sam was holding them.

He pulled her back until her shoulder-blades met the firm support of his chest, and wrapped both arms around her.

'Nothing, yet,' the medical director confirmed. 'I'll contact them again just before we start the afternoon session——' He broke off as Joan called his name and relayed a message from the front of the plane. 'I'll speak to you later,' he said quickly as he hurried away.

'Keep your chin up,' Sam whispered.

'I'm trying, but. . .what if it doesn't arrive in time?' She twisted in the circle of his arms until she was facing him. 'The operation's been dangled in front of Chou like a carrot for a donkey, and it never seems to get any closer.'

'We're dealing with this sort of situation all the time, Sian. What makes this one so important?'

She was silent for a moment, weighing her words, then they burst out of her anyway. 'I just want to see him smile. . .' and a solitary tear made a silvery track down her cheek.

'None of that,' Sam chided, as he wiped all traces away with gentle fingers. His arm wrapped round her again to give her a comforting squeeze. 'Just remember the power of positive thought,' he encouraged, before it was his turn to scrub up for surgery.

Sian sat herself out of the way to watch Sam's next patient, but it was the surgeon who held her attention rather than the surgery he was performing.

As soon as the surgery was over, she decided that the walls were closing in on her and there were too many people around when she had so much to think about.

She escaped the close confines of the plane and set off for a brief stroll towards the boundary of the airport.

At one point she stopped walking and tilted her head back, her eyes tightly closed as she absorbed the sounds and the smells surrounding her. Even the air felt different, somehow, and she drew in a deep breath and held it before releasing it slowly.

Sam was right, she decided wearily. They dealt with these sorts of situations on a daily basis back home and she never let it get to her like this. It must just be Chou himself who was affecting her.

He was such a stoic, trying to support his grandfather and younger brother in spite of all his difficulties. But he was so solemn. . .

Sian gave herself a mental shake. If she carried on like this she would be in danger of developing a God complex. She certainly wasn't the only ophthalmic surgeon capable of performing the keratoplasty on Chou. There were three other surgeons arriving to join Orbis on Sunday and three more the week after that, apart from the many surgeons in Beijing itself.

If the cornea didn't arrive in time, at least she could console herself that Chou's eye condition had been investigated and a line of treatment recommended, so he was part-way towards success. . . Oh, but she would like to see the case through to its conclusion while she was still here. . .

Slowly, she turned around in a full circle, imprinting in her memory all the things she could see around her, pausing for a long time in contemplation of Orbis herself.

Even from a distance she was impressive, her white paint gleaming against the clear blue sky under the heat of the sun. The circular Orbis logo, with a stylised pair of hands holding the shape of an eye, showed up clearly on the tailplane, as did the internationally recognised sign of a red cross just in front of the rear door.

From here, the word 'ORBIS' painted on her side behind the front entrance looked small, but she knew that the letters were well over a foot high, the navy blue paint stark against the brilliant white.

As she watched, a figure detached itself from the

movement around the shadows under Orbis' fuselage
and started to come towards her.

'Sam,' she whispered, the breeze taking the word
from her lips and wafting it towards him even though he
was too far away to hear.

She waited, watching as he came closer, his long
athletic strides carrying him swiftly across the interven-
ing space.

As he came nearer, she could see that both his hands
were full, and she realised that he had collected a
packed lunch for each of them.

'Here.' He smiled as he held out the contents of one
hand. 'The best the hotel can provide.'

'Thanks.' She managed to retrieve the container of
drink and package of food without touching his hand,
rather disconcerted by the dark glasses he was wearing.
'They've managed to come up with something different
each day, so far.'

She looked at the container of drink with its lid firmly
in place, and then looked at her other hand holding the
food, before she glanced helplessly up at Sam to meet
his own amused expression.

'I'll make a bargain with you,' he offered. 'I'll hold
your food while you open your drink if you hold mine in
return.'

'Done.' She held out the carefully wrapped package,
then peeled off the lid before thirstily gulping down
nearly half of the fruit juice, her eyes closed in ecstasy
as the cool liquid slid down her throat.

'Hey!' He juggled the packages in front of her. 'Not
fair! I'm thirsty, too. Is that all the thanks I get for
bringing your food over?'

'I said I'd hold your food in return,' she confirmed.

'But I didn't say *when* I'd hold it. . .' She lifted the container up to her mouth again.

Before she could start to drink, Sam positioned his drink under hers and jiggled it so that the remaining liquid sloshed about and splashed her face and the lenses of her sunglasses.

She collapsed in helpless giggles and nearly spilt the rest of her drink.

'All right. All right,' she conceded, as she removed the sunglasses and wiped them, hooking one arm of them into the neck of her top before she held her hand out for the food parcels.

'What a grouch!' she teased as he started drinking, and watched the convulsive movements of his throat as he tilted his head back.

She tore her eyes away from the provocative sight and turned towards the plane, slowly starting the journey back to join the rest of the team in the shadow under her fuselage.

'Sian?' The gentle breeze blew the softly spoken word towards her and she paused to look back over her shoulder. 'If you're too hot out here, we could go back over there, but I thought it might be easier to talk where no one can overhear us?'

He had juggled with his double handfuls and had taken off his sunglasses, too, his dark eyes meeting hers candidly.

Her stomach took a dive, but she had to admit his idea was the perfect solution.

'OK.' She plastered a smile on tentatively, then straightened her shoulders firmly. 'You'll have to promise to hold my drink while I force an entry into my food, though.'

She held out the container, determined that he shouldn't know just how nervous she was.

'This is just like an awful department do at the hospital, where everyone is stuck with a drink and a plateful of food and needs a third hand to cope with getting anything into their mouth.' Sam laughed at their predicament as they swapped and juggled for a minute.

Finally, they had evolved a workable system and started eating.

'Shall we walk, while we eat?' Sian suggested, her nervous energy needing some kind of release, and they started pacing slowly, keeping parallel to the perimeter of the airfield.

For a long time neither of them spoke, but it was a comfortable silence, just as it had been when they'd had free time together when they were married.

'How's your little lad coping with the long wait?' Sam broke the silence at last.

'He must be getting awfully hungry but he's not complaining. He's just so resigned about it all—not in the least like a normal little boy. He should be full of mischief and fun and the only way you should be able to keep him still is by sitting on him!' Her voice was impassioned as she gestured with two hands full.

'You've obviously come across a lot who come into that category,' Sam laughed easily. 'What was it that made you specialise in paediatric ophthalmology? I don't remember you mentioning it when we were. . .'

'I didn't decide until after the divorce,' she confirmed quietly. 'I had several young patients whose problems should have been sorted out much sooner, or with more advanced techniques. Because of the delay, they've ended up with poorer vision than they should have, partly because there aren't enough paediatric speciality units.'

'So you decided to change the odds slightly?'

'In my own small way.' She raised her chin in a display of determination. 'And now that I'm on Orbis International's list I'll be able to help spread my own knowledge in countries where children are even worse off than at home.'

'It wasn't just a one-off idea, joining Orbis? You intend making it a regular thing?'

'Of course,' she replied, quite surprised at his question. 'Don't you?'

'Well, yes. But I thought you'd be too busy with your job to——'

'You know,' Sian interrupted, angrily stuffing the debris from her meal into the empty drink container, 'I can quite see why you had to take up some form of exercise after we separated. You always get enough exercise when I'm around just by jumping to conclusions.'

For a couple of seconds he was silent as her words registered, then the colour deepened along his cheek-bones before he struck back.

'You can't deny that you were the stereotypical career woman when I first met you. You were absolutely determined to get to the top of the ophthalmology tree as fast as possible.' His tone made the words sound like an accusation.

'So the fact that you were equally as driven to succeed was a point in your favour, whereas the fact that I'm a woman makes ambition a dirty word, does it?'

'When you allow it to ride roughshod over everything in its path, yes.' He glared down at her with turbulent eyes, his mouth closed into an unforgiving line as they continued walking in the strangely silent heat.

'Does that mean that you still think I put my career first?' she demanded heatedly, wrapping her arms around herself to control the shaky feeling inside. 'I expect you're still blaming me for losing the b-baby?'

She felt the warning sting in her eyes as her voice faltered, and blinked hard to dispel the gathering tears before she fixed her gaze firmly on the distant airport buildings, struggling to continue walking slowly and steadily.

There was a brief moment while they both gathered their thoughts after her emotional outburst, then Sam put one hand out to halt her and stepped in front of her to fix her with his solemn gaze.

'No,' he said firmly. 'I don't still blame you for losing the baby. I only blamed you when I thought you'd deliberately gone for an abortion without even talking to me about your decision.' He looked away over her head and gave a deep sigh. 'I suppose I was grieving and I was using you as the focus of my anger. . .'

His eyes returned to meet hers and she could see the difference in their expression. The bitterness had gone; only the remnants of sadness remained.

'As far as your ambition is concerned——' he smiled briefly '—just the fact that you're here with Orbis International would tell anyone that you're not just interested in climbing ladders.'

'It's one of those jobs where you're happy to be paid in smiles rather than money,' Sian agreed, smiling openly as a wave of happiness slowly filtered through all the empty spaces inside her.

Finally, she repeated the question she'd first asked the night before.

'Sam?' She put one hand over his, where it rested on her forearm. 'Where *do* we go from here?' She drew in a deep breath before she continued, tentatively, 'Do you think there's a chance that we'll get back together again?'

It was a long time before he spoke, and the longer it became, the lower Sian's heart sank.

'I don't know if I'm ready for a commitment,' he said, his words typically blunt. 'I don't know if I'll ever be ready——'

'But——'

'But I do know I've missed you.' He slid his empty hand down her arm and took hold of her hand.

'Have you?' she whispered huskily, her blue eyes huge as she gazed up at him.

'God, yes.' He squeezed her hand. 'I never realised before how empty a room can be when there's only one person in it and there used to be two.'

'You're still living in the same house?' She couldn't hide her surprise. She had often wondered where he had moved to after the divorce.

'I tried to tell myself it was inertia that kept me there, that I didn't have time to go house-hunting for the sake of it when I was living in a perfectly comfortable house already, but. . . I suppose if I'm really honest, I'd have to admit that I just didn't want to move. There were too many memories that I didn't want to leave behind. . .'

'I've moved twice, since then,' Sian admitted. 'Nowhere seems like home after living in that house. . .' She closed her eyes, her words replaying in her head and, as she heard the silent plea in them, she felt the heat spread in her cheeks.

'Do you live very far away now?' Sam seemed to be

oblivious to the undercurrent in her words. 'Perhaps you want to come back. . .'

'Oh, Sam!' Happiness blazed through her at his words. 'I'd love to.'

'. . .for a visit.'

There was a dreadful silence as they first gazed at each other in horror and then avoided each other's eyes.

'Ah, Sian, I only. . .'

'Oh, Sam. I'm so sorry. . .'

Their words trailed away as they had done so often in the past, but this time there were no smiles or laughter.

'I'm sorry, I misunderstood,' Sian said stiffly through her embarrassment.

'I only meant for you to visit the house if you wanted to.' He was obviously uncomfortable and trying to find enough words to smooth over her blunder. 'You put a lot of work into restoring it and sorting out the décor, and never had a chance to see the finished job.'

'Thank you for the offer,' she said politely. 'I'll see if I can fit in a visit some time.' She managed to force the words out, even though her throat was nearly closed with the effort of holding back the tears of mortification.

'Sian, I can't. . .' He shook his head. 'You know I'm attracted to you. Hell, it's been almost impossible for me to keep my hands off you since we've been in Beijing.' His dark eyes seared her with their intensity and she started to quiver deep inside.

It shamed her to realise that even as he was rejecting her he could still arouse her with nothing more than a look, but she was powerless to resist.

'If we're being honest with each other, we've come pretty close to making love already and it wouldn't take much for us to tear each other's clothes off here and now in spite of the fact we'd have an audience.' One side of his mouth quirked up in a self-deprecatory grimace.

'Oh, let's be brutally honest, by all means,' Sian retorted, burying her embarrassment with her foolish dreams under an avalanche of sarcasm and anger. 'Why not admit that you'd like nothing better than a willing partner in bed just as long as she didn't get any stupid ideas about commitment. It would certainly be cheaper than having to pay a prostitute for relief of those inconvenient male urges, and there's so much less chance of catching something nasty.'

She turned on her heel and started striding back towards Orbis. For the first time in her life she was far too angry for tears.

How dared he? How dared he think she would be satisfied with the occasional romp in bed? She loved him, for heaven's sake, the narrow-minded, short-sighted——

'Hey!'

Suddenly she was grabbed by one elbow and swung to a halt.

'Dammit, Sian. Don't you dare spout off such a load of garbage and then expect to storm off in high dudgeon.' He was angry enough to spit fire, his jaw rigid and his mouth grim.

'You know damn well I didn't mean it that way——'

'Do I?' she challenged. 'In one breath you're telling me you want my body any way you can get it, and in the next, you're telling me I can come to the house we used to live in together, but only as a visitor to have a look at the décor. You tell me what that sounds like—or did I miss something?'

He released her elbow and bent to retrieve the debris from his meal, crushing it between powerful hands.

'It sounds like the words of a man who doesn't know if he can trust himself again,' he said finally, his voice very low and the words full of anguish.

'What do you mean?' Sian was riveted by such an admission from someone who always seemed so sure of himself—of who he was and where he was going. 'It was me you didn't trust, when you thought I'd killed our baby. Now that you know it wasn't. . .'

'No.' He shook his head sadly. 'I lost my trust in my own judgement. First, when I believed you were capable of doing such a thing and now, that I could have even thought you would do it.'

'Oh, Sam. You've trapped yourself in a Catch-22 situation. We're damned if I did and damned if I didn't. So what happens next?'

A piercing whistle broke the stillness of the early afternoon and they both looked over towards Orbis.

Several of the small figures which were other members of the team were waving at them.

'Come in, number two, your time's up,' Sam quipped, as they started walking briskly towards the plane. 'It must be time for the afternoon patients.'

Sian murmured a wordless agreement and matched her pace to his. Her heart was heavy inside her, but at least they had finally laid all the lies to rest.

Even though they would still be apart, the bitterness at his unjust accusation would now be able to disperse. Perhaps, one day. . .

'Sian. . .'

They were halfway back to the plane when the thin sound of a voice carried to her.

She stopped for a second and concentrated hard on the gesticulating figures.

'Sam. Something's wrong. . .' She took off her sunglasses and shaded her eyes in the hope of seeing more clearly. 'That's Joan, and the medical director. . .' and she took off at a run, her feet flying over the hot tarmac in a direct line towards Orbis.

Sam reached the reception committee first, but Sian wasn't far behind.

'It's coming,' Joan carolled delightedly, her face wreathed in smiles.

'Chou's cornea will be here this afternoon,' the medical director confirmed, and Sian burst into tears.

CHAPTER NINE

'IDIOT!' Sam chided as he picked Sian up and swung her round in a circle to the accompaniment of cheers. 'You shouldn't be crying!'

'I'm not!' Sian objected, a stream of silvery drops raining down her cheeks. 'I'm happy!'

'Women,' he growled as he finally allowed her feet to touch the ground and supported her until she stopped swaying. 'Cry when they're sad, cry when they're happy. What's a mere man supposed to do?'

'Mere man?' she muttered under her breath as the other men commiserated with him. 'You've never been a mere man in your life. . .'

'A compliment?' he murmured, his eyes gleaming secretively at their private sparring. 'Careful, I might get the wrong impression. I might think you like me. . .' and he winked at her before he left her to talk to the medical director, while he prepared to give his final talk before the afternoon surgery began.

'Now that you've got your feet back on the ground,' the medical director teased, 'I finally had confirmation that a cornea is being sent over and should arrive later this afternoon.'

'Did they give any idea what time?' Sian prompted, and glanced at her wrist, quite forgetting she wasn't wearing her watch.

'They hope it should be here by four,' he confirmed. 'That will give us time to get Chou prepped and ready as soon as the last case on the list is finished.'

'How firm is that?' she queried in a worried voice. 'I'd hate to tell Chou and his grandfather that it's coming and then it didn't arrive.'

'The only thing that's tentative is the time of arrival,' he promised. 'It's coming from the second eye bank and will have to travel across Beijing.'

'Is there any cut-off time as far as Orbis is concerned?' Sian asked. 'I know there are official things happening this evening, but is there any time beyond which the operation can't take place?'

'No,' he laughed. 'On odd, exhausting occasions we have been known to work right through the evening, but we don't like to make a habit of it. No one can do their best work if they're dead on their feet.

'As far as the official function is concerned, it's more of an Orbis-only affair this evening, with just the resident team, the visitors and guests.

'As far as our Chinese hosts are concerned, they're very understanding because they've had us here before and they know that delays can happen. If you don't finish in time to join us, I promise I'll make your apologies.

'Now——' he smiled encouragingly '—go and pass the news on to your patient, then check up on your team of happy volunteers.'

Sian raced up the steps effortlessly, her heart light and her excitement building as she entered the plane in search of an interpreter.

Tears threatened again when the news was broken to Chou and his grandfather.

Chou took the news so calmly that for a moment Sian wondered if he had understood what the interpreter was telling him. His grandfather held his hand out towards

Sian, and when she placed her own in it, he squeezed it tightly between his own without saying a word.

Everyone on the plane had heard that the cornea was coming, and there was an almost festive atmosphere as the operating theatre was prepared for the final session of the week.

'It's almost as if it's happening to a member of the family,' Sian commented in amazement. 'For us visitors, I could understand it, but the resident team must see this happen time and time again.'

'Not quite like this,' Joan explained. 'For some reason, Chou's situation has touched everyone's heart. You should have heard us when the call came through to say there was a cornea available for him. The whole team cheered. I'm surprised you and Sam didn't hear us right across the airfield,' she finished with a smile.

'I've been checking back with each of the people who volunteered to work late, if we got the go-ahead.' Sian consulted her list. 'Now, the only person missing is my number two. There isn't a host doctor scheduled to assist because the operation wasn't on the list.'

'Pencil my name in,' a deep voice said behind her, and she turned to face Sam.

'You want to assist?' Sian queried in amazement. 'But. . .'

'I doubt you'll need me for anything important,' he said calmly, 'but I'll be there, just in case,' and he held her gaze, his dark eyes speaking volumes.

Sian caught the soft flesh inside her lower lip between her teeth while she fought for control, and drew in a sharp little breath.

'Thank you,' she whispered. 'I. . . 'Thank you,' and she smiled tremulously up at him.

When the cornea finally arrived in its insulated carrier

just after four that afternoon, it was welcomed with a cheer.

The last scheduled operation of the day was nearly completed when Chou and his grandfather were escorted up the steps and into Orbis, the interpreter explaining in simple terms what would be happening to prepare Chou for surgery.

The eleven-year-old's impassive mask finally cracked, to reveal the uncertain child hiding inside, when the intravenous line was hooked up. For the first time he reached out to hold tight to his grandfather, only releasing his gnarled hand when the pre-med took effect.

Sian was able to arrange a seat for Chou's grandfather so that, although his own blindness would prevent him from watching his grandson's operation, he would be able to hear the translation by the interpreter.

'The interpreter must have told the visitors in the class-room what was going on,' Liz informed Sian as she and Sam went through to start scrubbing. 'They've all sat down again in their seats to wait to watch Chou's surgery.'

'And Gavin's going to be recording just as if this one was on the original list,' Ann chipped in.

'That will solve one problem for the medical director, then,' Sian laughed. 'If our hosts are here watching the operation, they'll be just as late for the official function tonight as we will,' and she held her hands out for the disposable gloves to be snapped into position over the bottom edge of the sleeves of her gown, then covered with large plastic bags.

'Ready?' Sam murmured through his mask.

'As I'll ever be,' she replied, her eyes shining up at him. 'Thanks for your support. It means a lot,' and she pushed her way through the heavy doors and into the operating-room.

She settled herself quickly and positioned the operating microscope before the plastic bags were removed.

'Good afternoon, ladies and gentlemen. Our patient is an eleven-year-old boy. His sight is irrecoverable in one eye, but we are hoping to save the other eye this afternoon by replacing his damaged cornea with a graft from a healthy donated cornea.'

She focused on the field of operation and continued her introduction.

'As you can see, the patient is under general anaesthetic because of his age and the length of time the operation will take. The eye has been immobilised by injection, and the top and bottom eyelids held open.'

She brought the donated cornea into focus. 'The graft will be the full thickness of the cornea and about seven millimetres in diameter.'

As the operation progressed, she detailed the process of trephining, in which Chou's cornea had a circle cut out of the centre, almost as if she were using a miniature pastry-cutter.

'The disc of cornea is left in position until the last minute, to prevent infection and loss of the contents of the chamber behind the cornea.' She transferred her attention to the donated cornea.

'We now cut an identical disc from this cornea and replace one with the other.' She suited her actions smoothly to her words, adding as she did so, 'Because the cornea doesn't require a direct blood-supply, there is little risk of rejection of the graft. And even if it did become opaque, the keratoplasty can always be repeated.'

While she was speaking, she had positioned the disc

exactly inside the aperture left by the removal of Chou's almost opaque cornea, and was ready for the next stage.

'The graft must be sutured smoothly in position, with even tension maintained around it. This is easiest if the stitches are placed evenly, for example, like the figures on a clock-face. If you start with one at twelve o'clock and one at six, then one at three and one at nine, you can then space the other stitches between these to keep the tenson right.'

She painstakingly placed the last suture and made a final check that the join didn't have any leaks, before removing the instrument holding the lids open and taping a dressing in position.

She straightened up to make her closing remarks, and couldn't find the strength to speak; her throat was closed by the emotions welling up in her.

Out of sight of the camera, Sam took hold of one hand and held it tight while his deep voice took over.

'Chou will be transferred to the hospital now, and will be seen tomorrow and checked again before the stitches come out. Hopefully, he won't need to be seen again.'

At intervals throughout the surgery there had been questions from the doctors in the class-room, and Sian had become accustomed to the two-way communication. The sound she could hear now had her puzzled until Sam explained.

'They're applauding,' he murmured quietly, and guided her through to the scrub-room before he stripped off his gloves and reached out to remove her mask.

She stood as passively as a tired child while he removed her gown and then his own, until finally they stood in their pale blue scrubs and booties.

'Come here,' he murmured gruffly, as he held his

arms out to her and she stepped into them, her head coming to rest against his shoulder as if it belonged.

The world receded until all that mattered was bounded by two strong arms wrapped firmly around her, holding her tightly against the muscular wall of his chest. His heartbeat sounded loud in her ear, the steady beat as regular and timeless as forever.

The tension which had been building in her, ever since she had met Chou and recognised his plight, slowly drained away, leaving an almost euphoric calmness in its stead.

'Right, Cinderella,' Sam's voice laughed down at her, drawing her back to the present. 'I remember you telling me that, on Orbis, the surgeons have to clean their own floors and sinks. Shouldn't you be pactising what you preach?'

He was smiling as she finally met his eyes, and she realised that she wouldn't have wanted to share this moment, this emotion, with anyone else.

Maybe, when he resolved his feelings, he would decide that he didn't want to get married again. The thought was painful, especially as she had realised the depth of her own feelings for him. The only consolation was that it seemed as if they were at last developing the start of the friendship which hadn't had time to develop before.

'All right, my trusty assistant.' She stepped back from him, missing the contact between their bodies as if she had lost a part of herself. 'Come and assist with the mucky jobs,' and she led the way towards the cleaning supplies.

'Too late,' Joan smiled. 'Clean-up's finished and we're all just about ready to lock up. It's time to get back to the hotel to put our glad rags on,' and she ushered them through to change out of their pale blue scrubs for the last time.

The last official function was the meeting organised by Celia in the same small conference-room where the team had all met for the first time less than a week ago.

'It's incredible that so little time has passed,' Sian marvelled. 'It seems as if I've known everyone for ages.'

'That's part of the magic of Orbis,' Joan said happily. 'Every three weeks we go to a different country and every week we meet different surgeons, nurses, technicians, and by the time we part, they're all part of the Orbis family.'

'Ladies and gentlemen.' Celia called them to order with her customary ease. 'If I could have your attention for one last time. . .?'

Within a minute everyone was seated, Sam pulling Sian into the adjoining seat to his.

'The first-time visitors will probably have noticed that the resident team on Orbis all wear a little set of wings on the lapel, incorporating the Orbis logo.' She indicated the gold-coloured emblem on her jacket.

'This is the point where each of the new members is presented with their own set of wings as a souvenir of their first mission on Orbis,' and she completed a roll-call of all the visiting team for the medical director to present each one personally with an individual memento.

'It's just a small token,' he said, when they had all received them, 'but it is visible proof that you have all been part of the Orbis dream.'

For about an hour the group remained chatting with the ease of long-time friends, exchanging anecdotes and gossip, with promises to keep in touch.

'Has anyone still got presents to buy for family and

friends back home?' Joan enquired of the group containing Sam and Sian. 'Silk Street is within walking distance of the hotel, just along the main avenue. Several of us are going to have a look, and you're welcome to come along.'

There was a chorus of 'goodnight' and 'see you in the morning' to those remaining behind, as their party made their way out of the room and took the lift for the ground floor.

'There's a food market on China Avenue, near the Beijing Sheraton,' Joan told them, as they made their way along streets that were still crowded in the early-evening light. 'It's full of stalls offering local foods actually cooked on the stalls. The mixture of smells is absolutely amazing, but we never recommend that Orbis staff eat there, just in case anyone ends up with an upset stomach.'

'I don't suppose Orbis can carry enough spare staff to cope with any sort of epidemic if a group was to try something that disagreed with them,' Sian suggested.

'Exactly,' Joan agreed. 'It's a shame to come so far from home and have to stick to hotel food, but it's much safer in the long run.'

They turned into Silk Street and before they scattered, arranged a time to meet at the same spot.

'Are you looking for anything in particular?' Sam asked roguishly. 'Underwear? Nightdresses?' He waggled his eyebrows at her suggestively.

'I was actually thinking of looking at some blouses or shirts.' Sian tilted her nose in the air in mock disdain. 'I've heard that some of the embroidery is fantastic. . .'

'Spoilsport,' he muttered, as they wandered along among the crowds.

Some of the stalls sold cotton goods, ranging in type

from ordinary household quality to high-fashion goods, but it was the silk that caught Sian's eye.

'Oh, Sam. Look. . .!' She was drawn irresistibly towards a display of shirts in a rainbow of pastel shades. 'It's so soft. . .and so fine,' she admired, as she stroked the fabric closest to her and discovered she could almost see her fingers through it.

She was entranced as the stallholder invited her to touch each of the fabrics, pointing out the different weights and thicknesses and showing his own favourites, without either of them understanding a word the other said.

When she had finished paying for her choice and had accepted the carefully wrapped parcel, she turned to look for Sam.

For a moment she couldn't see him, in spite of his impressive height and size among the generally shorter Chinese surrounding her. As she turned in a circle, she suddenly caught sight of him making his way towards her, and her heart gave a happy leap at the sight of his smiling face.

'Anything else you want to get?' he enquired, looking very pleased with himself.

'Don't tempt me,' Sian groaned. 'I could happily spend a fortune in here without any trouble.'

'Did you get what you wanted?' He glanced briefly at the slim gold watch he had strapped on before they left the hotel.

'I hope so. She did her best to look mysterious. 'I'll let you tell me when we get back to the hotel.'

'If you've finished buying up Beijing, we could go back to the hotel, if you like. I told Joan not to bother to wait for us.' He slid his hand under her elbow to guide her back in the direction of the hotel.

They didn't talk much, content to watch the bustle of Beijing going about its everyday life and point out interesting cameos to each other.

'You might as well have the bathroom first,' Sam suggested as they reached their room. 'I'd like to sort a few things out first,' and he took his jacket off and went over to the wardrobe.

Sian happily picked up her nightwear and disappeared towards the other room. She was enjoying the new relaxed atmosphere beween them, knowing that they had managed to lay some of their ghosts to rest in the last few days.

'Just going down to Reception for a minute,' he called round the door. 'Shouldn't be long. . .'

Refreshed and sweetly scented, Sian came out into the bedroom wearing just her nightie, and saw Sam's suitcase sitting on the little rack at the side of the wardrobe, his clothes placed in neat piles inside it.

'You always were much neater at packing than I am,' she muttered to the absent Sam, while she tried to hide the parcel containing the shirt she had chosen for him without disrupting his other belongings.

Her heart contracted with a sharp pang at the visible reminder of the brevity of their stay. 'I won't be doing mine till the last moment tomorrow. . .'

She was wondering what suggestions Sam would have for their last morning in Beijing, when she noticed the parcel he had put on her bed.

Her fingers were shaking slightly as she untied the neatly knotted string and unwrapped the paper.

'Oh,' she breathed, as a shimmering waterfall of silvery cream silk, slid through her fingers.

She held it up by delicate straps and saw what seemed to her to be the most beautiful nightdress in the world.

The silk was as fine as cobwebs, with a sheen to it that reminded Sian of the lustre on a pearl.

She couldn't resist trying it on, discarding her fine cotton for the sensuous slither of silk, as she drew it over her head and allowed it to drift in folds around her slender legs.

The cut was deceptively simple, clinging and flowing over her body apparently seamlessly, shamelessly outlining the curve of her hips and the jut of her pert breasts.

She heard the sound of the key in the lock too late to retreat to the bathroom, and was caught like a doe in the headlights of a car when Sam opened he door.

Her first reaction was to try to hide her body, and her hands came up to shield herself in a gesture as old as time.

'Oh, God.' The words were half-curse, half-prayer as he closed the door behind him and leant back against it as if his legs had lost their strength.

His eyes travelled over her from head to foot, the expression on his face telling her as clearly as any words that he liked what he saw.

It was the look in his eyes which gave her the courage to draw her hands away from their defensive position and leave her exposed to his gaze.

'Sweetheart,' he whispered achingly. 'I hope you know what you're doing to me. . .' He straightened away from the door and prowled slowly towards her, his hands tightly clenched and his eyes constantly roving over her as if charting the evidence of her growing arousal.

'If it's anything like what you're doing to me. . .' she started boldly, the words fading away to nothing as he came to a halt in front of her, mere inches separating their bodies.

One hand came up and one fingertip traced the line of the strap as it curved over her shoulder to join the nightdress just above the swell of her breast, then followed the shape of the neckline as it dipped into the shadow between them.

'Sam,' she whispered, the single word a plea from her heart as she looked up into the dark fire of his eyes.

'What do you want, Sian?' His voice was gravelly as his breathing became rougher. 'Tell me what you want.' His hand was visibly trembling as it hovered over the curve of her breast.

'You,' she breathed, cupping her hands around his cheeks with the touch of butterflies' wings to draw him down towards her. 'I want you, Sam. . .' and she touched her parted lips to his and arched her body towards him.

Their mouths met and her eyes closed helplessly as she moved into his arms, unable to stay out of them for a moment longer.

With that single kiss he seemed to take her over, make her part of himself, her mind, her body, her very soul opening up to him and absorbing him in turn.

'Sian,' he whispered against her burning mouth as he swept her off her feet, cradling her tightly against the hammering of his heart as he carried her across the room to his bed.

The kiss was broken when he lowered her feet to the rich pile of the carpet, and Sian lifted heavy lids to gaze up into eyes dark with passion, fierce with arousal.

She closed her eyes again and tilted her head, exposing the slenderness of her throat to his possession as her muscles turned to liquid. She clutched at his waist, her fingers curling around the soft fabric of his shirt for support before they burrowed beneath to find the sleek, hard muscles of his back.

They were kissing so fervently that she was hardly aware when he shed his clothes, only knowing when he pulled her close again to stroke his naked body against the silky second skin covering her own.

'This is what I thought of doing when I bought it for you.' His deep voice was husky with arousal. 'I imagined myself seeing your shadowy shape through the softness, the curve of your breasts waiting for the touch of my hands.' He cupped her as he whisperd the words against her lips.

'I imagined your nipples becoming aroused against the fineness of the silk and making little peaks in the fabric—just like this.' He directed her gaze to her own tumescence as he outlined them with his fingers. 'Then, I thought of how the silk would become transparent and cling if I took them in my mouth. . .'

She moaned aloud as the wet heat of his tongue met her nipples, as he licked and suckled them in turn through the tantalising silken barrier.

'Sam. . .' she groaned as she clung to his shoulders, her legs no longer capable of supporting her.

She revelled in the feel of him, her fingers exploring the powerful muscles under the hot satin of his skin as the warm clean scent of him surrounded her in a sensual, musky aura. She swayed towards him, almost dizzy with arousal, and cradled his dark head against her pale breast, while he buried his face against her.

'Please. . .' She didn't know what she was begging for, but Sam seemed to know as he lowered them both on to the cool smoothness of the bed.

'I imagined. . .' He lifted his head to watch his fingers

stroke her with feathery caresses over her shoulder and down her arm. 'I imagined looking at your shadowy secrets through the silk, the shape of your hip and the curve of your stomach. . .'

The tiny hairs on her skin quivered as he outlined each of them, his touch barely disturbing the fine silk.

A dark heat started pooling deep inside her as she saw his stormy gaze finally reach its ultimate goal.

'I tried to visualise how you would look, here——' his fingertips strayed lower '—with the silk trying to hide your dark womanliness from me.' His touch became more intimate, searching out the moist petals that were softer than the finest silk.

'Sam, please. . .' She arched helplessly against his hand, her thighs parting for him as she reached across to explore his dark masculinity, cupping him intimately as she urged him to slide his body over hers.

He shut his eyes tight, dropping his head back and groaning aloud as she stroked his rigid length. He resisted her efforts just long enough to sweep the hem of her nightdress up to her waist, then settled himself over her at last.

Slowly, he took possession of her, his eyes meeting hers in blatant masculine triumph when he felt the tell-tale tightness.

'Mine,' he growled fiercely, as he sank himself to the hilt in her velvet depths.

The world receded until all that existed was the two of them, and she arched to meet him, welcoming him and urging him deeper and deeper, wrapping herself around him until they were one.

Her hands explored his heated skin with a will of their own, tracing the power and breadth of his shoulders, the lean length of his back and the taut rhythm of his hips as he moved above her and in her.

Finally, when she thought she would die of pleasure, he surged against her one last time and forced them both into a cataclysmic explosion.

In slow stages, the world came back into focus, Sam's body a beloved weight on her own, his shoulder salty against her lips and tongue, the muscles of his back clearly defined in spite of his boneless state of relaxation.

He drew in a deep breath, and Sian silently mourned the end of their wordless closeness as he lifted his head, supporting his weight on his elbows.

'I've had to wait two years for this,' he murmured softly, his eyes darkly intent as he lifted one finger to trace her kiss-swollen lips.

'Two years?' Sian wondered what he meant, but his finger was exploring the slick inside of her lower lip and the edge of her teeth in a delightful distraction. 'What do you mean, you had to wait. . .?' Her eyebrows drew together as she tried to concehtrate.

Dark colour tinged Sam's cheekbones as he dipped his head and bathed her lips with his tongue, almost as if he wanted her to forget what he'd said.

'Oh!' Her eyes grew wide as his words finally made sense. 'You can't mean. . . You haven't made love to anyone since the divorce?' Her tone was incredulous 'But. . . I don't understand. Why not? You're a very sexual man and you could virtually take your pick of the available women. . .'

The colour darkened, suffusing his throat and face.

'Thanks for the vote of confidence,' he drawled in a husky voice, his eyes doing anything but meet hers. 'Unfortunately, my body doesn't agree.'

His mouth snapped shut as if he regretted allowing the words to escape, and he rolled away from her to lie on his back, his hands linked under his head as he gazed up at the ceiling.

Sian slid across to him, propping her head up on one hand to admire his leanly muscular perfection, while the other hand toyed idly with the silky whorls of dark hair scattered across his chest.

As she ran her fingers through it she encountered one tightly budded nipple, and leant forward to anoint it with her tongue.

'Do you mean to tell me,' she whispered smugly, her face wreathed in a wicked smile as she lifted herself up to straddle the evidence of his renewed arousal, 'that this only happens for me. . .with me. . .?' and she covered him completely with her body.

'Yes. . .' he hissed ecstatically against her mouth, as he held her face between his hands and arched his hips convulsively upwards.

At some time during the night Sam had roused her to slide under the covers, then he'd joined her there, and it was a long time before they finally went back to sleep.

Sian lay with her head pillowed on his shoulder, Sam's arm wrapped firmly around her waist even as he fell asleep as suddenly and deeply as a child.

She turned her head slightly to press a soft kiss to his chest right over his heart.

'I love you,' she whispered into the darkness. 'Oh, Sam, I love you.'

She smiled softly as she tried to make out his features in the gloom, her physical contentment no match for the soul-deep happiness which filled her.

Sam loved her. She knew it, not because he had said

the words, but because he had shouted it aloud with every passionate move he had made.

When they woke in the morning they would have so much to talk about, to plan.

Suddenly, she couldn't wait to start the rest of her life.

A picture crept into her mind, the sort of wishful thinking which just a week ago would have seemed impossible, but now. . .the image of the two of them living together once again in the house they had worked on together. Perhaps a child. . .?

One hand crept beneath the covers and came to rest beside his broader palm where it lay in repose over the soft hollow of her belly and she went to sleep with a gentle smile on her face.

CHAPTER TEN

SIAN woke slowly, and lay contentedly reliving the events of the past night.

She put one hand out to reach for Sam, missing the close contact with his body, but the other side of the bed was empty and cold.

'Sam?' She rolled over sleepily to look towards the bathroom, thinking he might be there, but the door was open and the room was silent.

'He can't have gone down to breakfast without me?' she said indignantly. 'We could have splashed out and ordered from room service. . .' She dropped back against the rumpled pillows with a disgruntled expression on her face at the lost opportunity.

They could have eaten their breakfast in bed and then, while they decided what to do until it was time to get ready to go to the airport for their flight home, they could have. . .

She sat up hastily, cutting her wanton daydreams off abruptly as she gazed around the room again for confirmation of her sudden suspicions.

Tugging the sheet free from the tangle of crumpled bedclothes, she wrapped it around herself as she made her way across the room to the wardrobe.

It was empty.

She closed the doors and turned to lean back against them as she surveyed the rest of the room. It was all gone. Everything of Sam's had disappeared as completely as if it had never been there at all.

Sian staggered into the bathroom, tripping over the trailing sheet, and caught the clean scent of his soap and shampoo hanging in the air, but everything had gone from there too, just his neatly folded towel left on the vanity unit beside the basin.

She reached out and picked it up, feeling the dampness remaining in it, and brought it up towards her face to draw in the lingering mixture of scents that represented Sam's presence.

The tears started to gather behind her eyes and tighten her throat as she went back to the bedroom.

Somewhere, there must be a note. He wouldn't have just gone without letting her know. . .

A thorough search of any likely place, and several unlikely ones, failed to reveal any trace of a message.

She buried her face in the towel, fighting hard not to give in to the heart-break which was hovering over her.

For several long moments she fought for control, telling herself that it would be wrong to jump to conclusions. That was what had caused all the problems between them two years ago.

She stood up and straightened her shoulders resolutely, disapointment darkening her eyes as she took herself into the bathroom.

This was not how she had envisaged spending their last morning in Beijing, but as soon as she found out what had happened to Sam, they would be able to laugh about it together as they planned their new future together.

'Gone?' Sian queried, as if she doubted that the efficient young man behind the reception desk had understood her question properly. 'Where has he gone? When?'

'I am sorry,' he apologised politely. 'I do not know. I have only taken over at the desk this morning.'

'But. . .'

'I can only tell you that he has left the hotel.'

'Do you know what time he'll be back?' she persisted, a sick feeling of dread building inside her. 'What time is he due to pay his bill?'

'He has already paid for his bill, and for Mrs Dr Forrester.'

'I. . . Thank you,' Sian whispered, and turned away blindly, almost bumping into Philip and his wife.

'Hello, there,' he smiled in his usual friendly way. 'It's wonderful news about Chou's recovery, isn't it? Are you going to celebrate your success with a last trip around Beijing before it's back to the airport again?'

'No. . . I. . . No.' Sian shook her head, not quite certain what Philip had said or whether she had given a suitable reply.

'Are you feeling all right?' His wife took Sian's arm and led her across to one side of the reception area. 'You're looking awfully pale. You didn't eat something from one of the stalls last night, did you?'

'No. We. . . I ate in the hotel. I-I'm fine. Really.' She tried to gather her thoughts together before she made a complete fool of herself. 'I just came down to see when Sam left.'

'He went out on the first flight this morning,' Philip confirmed. 'It was the only one he could get at such short notice. . .'

Sian made her way back up to her room, not knowing whether she had said goodbye to Philip and his wife or not. All she could think about was escaping and hiding until the urge to scream out her agony had time to die.

After the night they had just spent together and the

most earth-shattering lovemaking of her life, Sam had
been in such a hurry to get away from her that he had
taken the first available flight this morning.

The pain in her heart was too great for tears as she sat
on the chair in front of the dressing-table mirror.

In the reflection she could see her own pale face, her
blue eyes darkening to slate as they caught sight of the
tumbled bedclothes behind her.

She closed her eyes tight to try to shut out the picture
of Sam's body lying on the bed with her, his arms
around her, his long hair-roughened legs tangled with
hers as they were joined together body and soul.

'No. . .' she moaned, and wrapped her arms tightly
around herself as she rocked backwards and forwards.

She didn't know how long she had been sitting in the
silence when she heard the sound of a key in the lock.

'Sam!' She turned towards the door, stumbling to her
feet in her haste to greet him. Philip must have been
wrong. . .

The door opened to reveal a flustered young hotel
domestic who had obviously been under the impression
that the room was empty and ready for cleaning.

She bowed politely in apology and pulled the door
shut very quietly.

Sian stared at the polished wood door for a long time
and realised that it was time to pull herself together.

She sat back down and concentrated, reaching deep
inside herself for the reserves of strength she knew she
could depend upon.

She would never have believed that the Sam she had
known would treat her like a cheap one-night stand. He
had obviously changed far more than she realised.

Well, far be it from her to chase after him, if that was
the way he wanted it. If all he had wanted was a no-

strings holiday affair, he should have told her. At least, if she had accepted his terms, she would have been prepared for him to leave.

Finally, she stood and braced her shoulders, looking straight at herself in the mirror.

'Every journey starts with the first step,' she quoted aloud, as she reached forward to open a drawer. 'It's time to get on with my life and the first step is to pack my bags.'

Sian returned to her job in the ophthalmic department of City Hospital, to colleagues who were agog with questions about her unusual 'holiday'.

The few close friends she had made since she had started to work there commented that she seemed rather subdued, but she sidestepped their concern with a light-hearted remark about jet-lag. After that, she made sure no one saw the struggle she was having to try to wipe Sam out of her mind and heart for a second time.

The days weren't so bad, when she was busy with the demands of a bustling paediatric ophthalmic department. Her young patients demanded all her concentration and patience.

It was the long, empty hours she spent away from the hospital that were the problem. Too many empty hours when she seemed unable to think of anything that didn't bring Sam to mind in some way or another.

Gradually, she lost her appetite and sometimes, even when she did make the effort to eat, her stomach refused to tolerate the food and she ended up running for the nearest bathroom.

The third time it happened, Sian took herself off to her GP to ask for tests to be done.

'I was very careful what I ate and drank while I was in Beijing and I took all my tablets religiously,' she reported. 'But I seem to have come back with some sort of bug and it's knocking the stuffing out of me.'

Her GP was a kindly man who listened quietly while he watched her nervous movements.

'It's not causing me any great problems, except my hands have started trembling by the end of the day, but I'm worried that I might have something catching and be risking my patients while they're in contact with me.'

He checked her over carefully, starting with the basics and ending by taking a blood sample and asking for a urine specimen.

'I'd like you to come back to see me in two days,' he suggested calmly. 'In the meantime, see if you can take things gently. Have you got any holiday entitlement left after your trip to China?'

'Well, yes,' she said reluctantly. 'But I don't really want to use it up just sitting at home.'

'Just two days,' he said firmly. 'You said yourself that you were worried you might be infectious. . .'

The two days couldn't pass quickly enough for Sian, the malaise seeming so much worse when she had too much time to think about it. She was tempted to go in to work just for half a day to relieve the monotony, but her sense of reponsibility towards her young charges wouldn't allow it.

Finally it was her turn to be called into the GP's surgery.

'Well?' she demanded anxiously. 'What's wrong with me? Is it contagious?'

The elderly man allowed himself a wry smile. 'Sometimes it seems like it,' he said cryptically, 'but no, your condition isn't contagious.'

'What did the tests show, then?' She watched as he tapped into his computer to call up the test results, muttering imprecations under his breath as he hunted for the right access code.

'You're slightly anaemic, you're run down and you're rather underweight, all of which are eminently treatable with a little time and common sense thrown in.'

'But——'

'All of these are minor conditions——' he overrode her interruption '—and could be attributable to the main condition.' He paused and looked at her over the top of his half-moon glasses. 'I take it you haven't yet realised that you're in the early stages of pregnancy?'

The silence was deafening, and Sian could hear her own blood roaring in her ears as the room started to whirl around her.

'Deep steady breaths,' a voice was intoning above her, as she gazed at the toes of her black leather shoes and realised that her head was being held between her knees.

'Lift your head up slowly,' he advised, as he supported her until she was once more leaning back in the chair.

'P-pregnant?' she squeaked. 'But. . .how?'

'Oh, in the usual way, I would expect,' he said drily, and Sian felt her cheeks flame with heat.

A baby! She and Sam were having a baby. . .!

'Is it all right? I'm not going to lose this one, am I? What should I be doing to——'

'Whoa!' he laughed. 'First things first. I take it you're pleased with the news? I wasn't certain at first when you keeled over like that.'

'Pleased?' She drew in a deep breath and allowed the thought to sink in. She was pregnant. With Sam's baby.

'Yes, I'm pleased. More than pleased. . .' and the corners of her mouth lifted into a smile for the first time in over a month.

'Good,' he nodded. 'In which case, I'll refer you to an obstetrician as soon as——'

'Why? What's the matter with the baby?' Blind panic coloured her voice at the thought that she might lose Sam's baby again.

'Calm down. You won't do either of you any good if you carry on like that,' he said sternly. 'I always refer my pregnant patients to an obstetrician. I hate getting out of bed in the middle of the night, then sitting around for the next dozen hours waiting for something to happen.' He was trying to sound grumpy but Sian could see the twinkle in his eyes.

'The practice nurse will give you a set of leaflets to read,' he said, while he tapped away at the keys on the computer again and the printer started its whining buzz. 'In the meantime, get yourself started on these vitamins and minerals and start feeding yourself up a bit.' He handed her the prescription form and added his final comment just as she was about to leave the room.

'It wouldn't do you any harm to let the baby's father pamper you a little. . .'

She managed to shut the doctor's words out of her mind until she got home again, when they returned with a vengeance.

In about seven months she was going to become a mother, but at the same time, Sam would become a father.

She sat down heavily on the side of her bed and thought back to that last night in Beijing. During their week together they had covered many topics in their various conversations, some nostalgic, some downright acrimonious with the accusations flying thick and fast.

Now she would have to find some way to contact him and let him know what had happened. She would have to tell him that she hadn't been using a contraceptive for two years and, if he asked why, she would have to be honest.

Once they had separated, there had been no point in taking anything as she had no intention of making love—how could she when Sam still held her heart?

She kicked off her shoes and padded around her tiny flat in her stockinged feet, finding fidgety things to do to occupy her hands while she tried to work out the best course of action.

A small heap of post had been delivered while she was out at the doctor's surgery, and she picked it up from the mat inside the door to sort through.

One envelope bore some exotic-looking franks over two Chinese stamps, the opposite corner of the envelope bearing the Orbis logo.

She retrieved the paper-knife from her writing-desk and slit the envelope open, wondering who had written to her.

Inside, there was a single sheet of notepaper, closely handwritten, and it was folded around a photograph.

Sian puzzled over the idenity of the happily smiling child for several seconds before she suddenly knew who it was.

'That's Chou!' she exclaimed aloud, and quickly scanned the letter to confirm her belief.

Joan had managed to take the photograph of Chou when he came back to visit the plane, after he had had his stitches removed and wanted to see everything properly.

'I know you said that one of the main reasons you fought so hard to organise the keratoplasty for him was because you wanted to see him smile, so here is the evidence. . .'

Sian gazed at the photograph until the young boy's outline blurred as her tears fell on to her hands.

'Oh, that smile was worth fighting for,' she whispered tearfully, wiping the tears away with the back of her hand.

It was an automatic reflex to want to show the photograph to Sam. He had known how badly she wanted the operation to succeed, and he had even stood in as assistant for the OR.

She walked through to her bedroom and propped the photograph on her bedside cabinet beside a favourite one of Sam, her own words echoing inside her head.

Worth fighting for. . . Worth fighting for. . .

She slid one hand over the flat plane of her belly and felt a deep conviction that she was making the right decision. Not only was it Sam's right to know about the baby they had created, but she was convinced that he would honestly *want* to know about the baby he had fathered, no matter how accidentally.

Sian reached over to pick up the photograph of Chou again, and smiled at his happy face.

'I'm taking you with me, Chou,' she murmured, as she put her shoes back on and retrieved her purse and keys. 'You can be the conversational ice-breaker. . .' and she let herself out of her front door.

Sian had been sitting outside Sam's consulting-room for over an hour and was becoming more and more nervous.

His receptionist had given her a speculative look, but

had agreed that it was neither necessary nor advisable to interrupt Sam's busy list for a social call, even if it was from his ex-wife.

Not that Sian had elaborated that far, just informing the inquisitive-looking woman that they had been colleagues at a previous hospital.

Finally, she heard his familiar footsteps coming along the corridor and the murmur of conversation as his receptionist informed him of his visitor.

He came round the corner and stopped in his tracks.

'Sian,' he said, and the lack of warmth in his voice pierced her to the core. 'This is a surprise. What can I do for you?'

'I had some news today and I thought you would be interested.' She kept her tone even, but it was a struggle. 'I had a letter from Joan—you remember, the head nurse on Orbis?—and she enclosed this photo.'

Sian held out the oblong towards him and he stepped forward to take it from her, coming to rest under the unforgiving light of a fluorescent tube.

He looks tired, she thought with a pang. His face is drawn and he's got dark circles under his eyes.

'Who's this?' He sounded as puzzled as she had been at first.

'Guess,' she suggested, and stood up out of her chair to look at the photograph over his arm. 'Don't you recognise my superb handiwork on that keratoplasty?' she teased.

His eyes met hers in amazement.

'This can't be that solemn little mite who never smiled once?'

'The very same.' She smiled broadly. 'How about that for a transformation?'

They both examined the photograph again before Sam glanced quickly at his watch.

'I'm sorry,' Sian apologised quickly, the gesture cutting her to the quick. 'I didn't mean to take up so much of your time. I just wanted to——'

'No.' He put one hand out to catch her elbow as she started to turn away. 'I was just checking the time before I asked you if you would like to join me for a drink. . .to celebrate.' He held up the photograph he still had in his other hand.

'Only if you're sure you have time,' she agreed, carefully trying not to show her elation.

'I just need to get my jacket.' He began to walk across the waiting area, then turned back towards her. 'I don't suppose you want to see my office?' he suggested.

'Not if it's terribly swanky,' she retorted pertly. 'Mine's a glorified shoebox decorated in Early Playgroup furniture.'

'Come and see.' He held out one hand to usher her through. 'My patients need grown-up furniture and I very rarely get original artwork from them to hang on my walls.'

His office was pleasant but unremarkable, except for the distant view he had from his window of one of the few trees in the area.

'A room with a view, no less,' she teased, then turned back to face him, finding a perch on the edge of the windowsill as he mirrored the action by settling himself on one corner of his desk.

Their smiles faded gradaually as they gazed at each other.

'You look tired. . .'

'How have you been. . .?' They both smiled wryly, then Sam spoke first.

'Neither of us looks as though we've enjoyed the last month or so,' he commented quietly.

'It hasn't been very easy,' Sian admitted. 'Especially the second time round.' She glanced around his room, recognising familiar scholarly works and periodicals, and the futility of their situation hit her all over again.

'Why did you go like that?' she demanded in a low voice. 'You must have known how it would make me feel. . .'

'What do you mean?' He looked so nonplussed that Sian errupted into speech in spite of her determination to remain calm.

'You treated me like a cheap one-night stand and sneaked off in the morning without so much as a farewell. How do you *think* I felt?' Her eyes started to burn with the threat of tears.

'No!' He exploded away from the desk to loom over her by the window. 'That's not true. I left a letter for you at the reception desk at the hotel.'

There was a long, horrified silence.

'Oh, God,' he groaned. 'You didn't get the letter. . .'

'No letter. No explanation. Nothing,' she confirmed.

'Oh, sweetheart, I'm sorry.' He lifted his hands as if he was going to hold her, but changed his mind at the last minute and let them drop by his sides again. 'What you must have thought of me. . .' He shook his head. 'It was partly your fault, you know.' He looked up from his contemplation of the floor with a lop-sided smile.

'*My* fault?' she queried indignantly. 'How. . .?'

'I didn't want to leave you after the fabulous night we'd just spent, and I delayed so long I nearly missed my plane. The taxi waited just long enough for me to scrawl a note to you to leave at the desk before we were risking life and limb to get to the airport on time.'

'What did the note say?' she queried, then added, 'I wish you'd woken me instead. . .'

'If I'd woken you up, you know full well what would have happened. I'd never have caught the plane!' He tentatively captured one hand and threaded their fingers together. 'It wasn't a love-letter or anything flowery.' He returned to her question again. 'It just said that I'd done some more thinking, and if you still wanted to see if we could make a fresh start, all you had to do was get in touch with me.'

'But when I didn't call, why didn't you ring me or something?' She was bemused by his strangely reticent behaviour.

'Unfortunately, I made the mistake of adding a final line which said something like, 'If I don't hear from you, I'll understand that you've changed your mind and I promise not to bother you. . .'

'You idiot!' She thumped him with her fist. 'You chose a very strange time to lose the courage of your convictions. Didn't it occur to you at some stage over the last awful month to contact me just on the off-chance I hadn't got your message?'

'I was getting there,' he admitted, as he finally took her in his arms to cradle her firmly against his chest. 'I'm just grateful that Joan sent you the photo of young Chou and you decided to bring it to show me.' One hand came up to cradle her head, his fingers threading through her hair.

'It's beginning to grow,' she murmured, as he stroked the softly curling strands, playing for time as she tried to find a way to broach the topic she knew she had to raise.

'You don't have to grow it for me,' he said seriously, tilting her head back so that he could see her face. 'I discovered that I like your hair any way you want to wear it. It's the person who matters.'

'Oh, Sam,' she whispered, and trailed her fingers down the side of his face to trace the lean contour of his jaw. Had their child inherited its father's jaw or. . .?

'I need to tell you. . .'

'I want to ask you. . .' This time the laughter was easier.

'What did you want to say?' Sian offered Sam the chance to speak first, but he paused for a moment, his eyes tightly closed as if he was steeling himself for a difficult task.

Finally his thick, dark lashes lifted to reveal turbulent dark eyes.

'I wanted to ask you. . .if you. . . Will you. . .? I want us to get married again. . . Please?'

Sian was breathless with shock, and everything inside her was urging her to say yes. But. . .

'Before I can give you an answer, I need to tell you something.' Her voice was qivering with tension as she gathered her courage, but still she couldn't bring herself to tell him baldly.

'Anything,' he offered. 'Ask me anything. Tell me anything. Only don't keep me in suspense.'

'In China,' Sian began, feeling her way, 'we admitted that we hadn't talked about whether we wanted a family and, if so, when we would want to start our family. . .'

'Sian——' he smiled indulgently '—I've discovered that it doesn't really matter whether we have children or not. The only thing that matters is having you.' He traced a line from her forehead and over her nose to her mouth, and she found herself pouting her lips in a kiss in spite of the worry growing inside her.

'So you'd rather not have any children?' she queried

in a hollow voice, feeling all her dreams slipping through her fingers.

'I'd love to have children,' he rejoined seriously, 'but it seems as if my body and mind have ganged up on me and said I can't have children if I can't have you. . .'

'But——' Sian tried to interrupt, but Sam placed one finger over her lips.

'. . .and if you'd rather dedicate yourself to your other children, then that's what we'll do.'

'Oh, Sam, I love you,' she whispered shakily. 'I'd love to marry you again, but only if. . .' She paused to take his hand in hers and place it over her belly. 'Only if you want our baby too.'

She looked up at him, her heart in her eyes, and saw his own eyes fill with tears.

'Oh, my love, I'd be delighted,' he managed to say in a husky voice just before he kissed her.

It was long moments before either of them surfaced from that kiss, and Sian could feel Sam's heart beating just as fast as hers.

'Of course, you realise I'm marrying you for your own good,' she murmured mischievously, as she smiled dreamily up at him.

'Why's that?' he said distractedly, as he nibbled his way gently towards her ear.

'Well, if I don't marry you, you're doomed to a life of celibacy. . .'

There was a long, stunned silence before he burst out laughing, filling his office with the joyous sound.

'You minx,' he chuckled, when he finally managed to control himself. 'Well, if you're the cure for what's wrong with me, I think this might be a good time for us to go to arrange for some therapy.'

He dropped a quick kiss on her mouth, then lingered for delicious seconds.

'I've got the feeling that this treatment is going to be good for both of us,' he murmured, as he retrieved his jacket.

'I won't argue with that.' She smiled up at him as he wrapped one arm around her and led her out of his room and along the corridor, both of them eager to leave the hospital.

The drive to the house they had once shared seemed endless, as Sian followed Sam's tail-lights through the heavy traffic and out to the quieter suburb.

Without thinking about it, they parked in their old places and walked up the path to the front door together.

Sam had his key ready to unlock the door, but before Sian could step over the threshold he swung her up in his arms and stepped through into the hallway, leaning back against the door to close it before he turned to carry her up the stairs.

'Sam!' she protested weakly, loving his display of masculine strength.

'Shh!' he whispered, bending to place a whimsical kiss on the tip of her nose. 'I've been dreaming of this for two years. Don't try to stop me now. . .' and he reached the top of the stairs and turned to enter the master bedroom.

'I wouldn't dream of stopping you,' she replied, feeling the slow awakening of her body as she thought of the pleasures to come.

'Good.' He smiled approvingly, as he placed her gently on the edge of the impressive double bed and started to remove her shoes.

Sian reached up to loosen his tie, and took her time

undoing the row of buttons on his shirt, revelling in the chance to run her fingers through the whorls of dark hair scattered over his chest as they were revealed through the open edges of his shirt.

The long month they had endured without each other had a predictable effect on their patience, and they knew that the leisurely pace couldn't last.

The last few garments were flung across the room in their race to uncover each other, finally to touch each other all over.

'Hurry,' Sian panted, as Sam fumbled with the zip at the side of her skirt, his hands less than steady after their forays over her naked breasts. 'I can't wait any longer,' she groaned, and she pulled him closer until his body covered her own and they became one.

'Oh, Sian, my love,' Sam chuckled, much later, when he finally found enough breath to speak. 'I'm so glad that we're finally seeing eye to eye.'

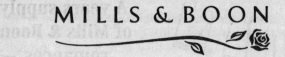

MILLS & BOON

LOVE CALL

The books for enjoyment this month are:

MIDWIFE'S DILEMMA	Lilian Darcy
MADE FOR EACH OTHER	Elizabeth Harrison
HOSPITAL AT RISK	Clare Lavenham
SEEING EYE TO EYE	Josie Metcalfe

Treats in store!

Watch next month for the following absorbing stories:

NEVER SAY NEVER	Margaret Barker
DANGEROUS PHYSICIAN	Marion Lennox
THE CALL OF DUTY	Jessica Matthews
FLIGHT INTO LOVE	Meredith Webber

Available from W.H. Smith, John Menzies, Volume One, Forbuoys,
Martins, Tesco, Asda, Safeway and other paperback stockists.

Readers in South Africa - write to:
IBS, Private Bag X3010, Randburg 2125.

A years supply of Mills & Boon romances — absolutely free!

Would you like to win a years supply of heartwarming and passionate romances? Well, you can and they're FREE! All you have to do is complete the word puzzle below and send it to us by 29th February 1996. The first 5 correct entries picked out of the bag after that date will win a years supply of Mills & Boon romances (six books every month—worth over £100). What could be easier?

GMWIMSIN

NNSAUT

ACEHB

EMSMUR

ANCOE

DNSA

RTOISTU

THEOL

ATYCH

NSU

MYSTERY DESTINATION

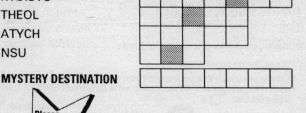

Please turn over for details on how to enter

How to enter

Simply sort out the jumbled letters to make ten words all to do with being on holiday. Enter your answers in the grid, then unscramble the letters in the shaded squares to find out our mystery holiday destination.

After you have completed the word puzzle and found our mystery destination, don't forget to fill in your name and address in the space provided below and return this page in an envelope (you don't need a stamp). Competition ends 29th February 1996.

Mills & Boon Romance Holiday Competition
FREEPOST
P.O. Box 344
Croydon
Surrey
CR9 9EL

Are you a Reader Service Subscriber?   Yes ☐   No ☐

Ms/Mrs/Miss/Mr _____

Address _____

_____

_____ Postcode _____

One application per household.

You may be mailed with other offers from other reputable companies as a result of this application. If you would prefer not to receive such offers, please tick box. ☐

COMP495
B